An Uncharted Journey
Into the Abyss

SPEAKING VOLUMES, LLC
NAPLES, FLORIDA
2020

An Uncharted Journey Into the Abyss

ISBN 978-1-64540-282-4

An Uncharted Journey Into the Abyss

John Tanner

Table of Contents

Jacinto 1

The Fortune Teller 13

Alfred the Mule.. 25

The Lost Explorers.. 49

The Lodge 59

Cry of the Ptarmigan...................................... 69

The Banjo Man 81

The Potter's Field 87

The Three Cards... 91

The Prospector 99

The Spy? 109

A Pirate's Affair.. 117

The Crow 123

Manifest Destiny... 129

A Turn of Events... 139

The Legend of Mi-Way-To............................. 159

194 Red Patch Road....................................... 167

The Midnight Murderer 179

Jacinto

Jacinto did not want to go to school. As usual, he had woken up early that morning to care for his small flock of sheep and cows, but he could still feel the pain from the fight he had been in the day before. It wasn't so much the physical pain that stung so much as the embarrassment from being called a poor immigrant and wetback. Before then, he had let the bully call him names and taunt him in front of his classmates, but at that point, he felt he couldn't take it any longer.

It was true that he was a small-boned child and part of a family of poor farmers just barely making a living, not to mention he had no father anymore, and his clothing was covered in patches. His face reddened just thinking about how Tomas had teased him all morning long before the school bell rang. That is, until he had swung his fist and squarely connected with the bully's nose. All the children around them heard the distinctive sound, like a piece of wood cracking, and soon enough, blood began gushing from the astonished boy's face. When Tomas felt the blood on his face, he began crying and immediately ran to the teacher, who sent them both to see the principal. Tomas had been a bully ever since Jacinto had known him. Tomas' father had money, maybe the most of anyone in the town, and owned a few local car dealerships, but as he got older, Tomas had gotten even more proud of his status and all the more aggressive.

The principal had spoken to them about what caused the fight, and they both had to sit in the detention room, although Jacinto could see a slight smile on the principal's face when he saw Mister Gonzalez look at him. When they were released from school that day, he had already heard the threats from Tomas and his friends. They were going to beat him up real good and run his family out of town.

It had felt good to finally fight back and punch Tomas, but now that they had threatened his family and their livelihood, it was a different matter. Even though he was only nine years old, he had not told his mother about the fight, not wanting to worry her. Even at this young age, he was seen as the man of the house. His chores included taking care of his little sister, for taking care of the livestock and tending to the family garden, as well as going to school. Meanwhile, his mother worked at a local restaurant—cleaning dishes and helping to serve customers—within the city limits of Deming, New Mexico, which was just across the border from the Sonoran Desert.

For ten minutes, he sat on his bed and wondered what the day would bring. He felt bad for having finally defended himself and was paralyzed with fear from the threats and repercussions that might follow him and his family. A thought popped in his head, making him wonder what they could do to him or his family and what resources they could use against him. They didn't have anything, and everyone at school knew Tomas' family had a lot of money, and with that money, they could employ the power of the local police and authorities. He was nervous and scared, and the worst part was that he felt powerless to do anything about it. Then, he remembered that the cows were waiting to be milked and the sheep needed to be led out into the pasture. They depended on him.

He jumped up from bed, grabbed a piece of hardened bread from the kitchen table and ran outside into the dark of predawn. As he began his morning chores, while biting down on the day-old bread, he made his way to the pen where the animals were kept. Immediately, he sensed something was wrong. The animals were huddled in two different corners of the pen and were silent. Looking out over the corral, he could see something, perhaps an animal, in the very middle. And it was not moving. He jumped down from the railing he had been standing on to get a better look and then, step by hesitant step, approached the animal. He could tell it was one of his baby lambs. Its legs were splayed out in all directions, and it had been partially eaten. Jacinto's heart sank even deeper into his chest. Now, not only had he brought problems to the family, but they had lost one of their precious lambs, of which they had very few. In a daze, he proceeded with his chores by milking the cows and bringing the sheep out to pasture, but with a sickening feeling that bordered upon dread.

After he was done, he went back to the pen to take care of the carcass. In the growing light, he could tell it was Fidel, one of his favorite lambs. Now, Jacinto was a tough boy and never feared hard work, but he felt the tears on his cheeks and could not stop them. His little friend was gutted, its entrails spread out across the sandy ground. Its face had been chewed on, and it appeared to have lost almost all of its blood. Whatever had killed him was a bastard of an animal, with a thirst for not only meat, but also blood. The thought that Tomas had something to do with this crossed his mind, but was quickly dismissed upon an examination of the lamb's injuries, which were very peculiar because typically, a coyote would drag its prey away rather than eat it in the pen, and not to mention, most of the meat was left intact. Maybe the coyote had rabies, and so he made sure to wear gloves when he buried his little lamb Fidel. He vowed to himself to kill whatever animal it was that had killed Fidel, and he would guard the pen if it came back to try and feast once more.

When he got to school, the other kids stopped talking when he passed by them. Something was different in the air. One girl, Maria, smiled broadly and wished him a good morning. Had she just flirted with him? When he saw Tomas and his friends, they all stopped talking, and a few of them shouted at him that he had better be ready to fight after school. Tomas, though, just looked mad and miserable.

At the end of the day, Jacinto quickly left after the bell rang and ran home. He knew he had enough problems with the flock and didn't want to get into any fights at school. When he got home, his mother looked worried. She could sense something was wrong. He let her know everything that happened that morning with one of their lambs, and with a grave look in her eyes, she brought out papa's old hunting rifle. Jacinto knew how to use the gun and had shot it a few times in the past. They only had five bullets left, so Jacinto would have to make sure he didn't miss.

That evening, after he had done his chores, he kept practicing sighting the rifle on different objects, pulling the trigger and hearing the empty ring of the gun. Later that night, as the shadows grew long across the barren, sandy outcropping that was their plot of land, he put a bullet into the gun and prepared some food and drink for the long evening outside. He had an apple, a peanut butter sandwich, and a canteen full of water, which he figured would last him the night. The animals appeared agitated. A couple of the sheep kept pacing the pen, while the baby lambs kept bleating with their eyes anxiously darting around. He surmised that they were uncomfortable with him being in the pen at that time of night, as he attempted to get comfortable for the long night ahead.

He decided the best way to kill the animal would be to stay in the pen with the animals overnight and cover himself with straw so that he not only would he be hidden from the beast, but also his smell would be masked. He gathered some straw and placed it in the corner of the pen so that he had a nice soft bed to sleep on. He stayed awake, looking at the stars and thinking about his day at school. Pretty brown-haired girl Maria had smiled at him, and it made his heart flutter to think of being with her. He also remembered how his schoolmates had looked at him differently once they realized that he wasn't going to put up with Tomas and his friends teasing him. Then there was the thought of the angry faces of Tomas and his friends. They wanted revenge and were plotting how they would get him back. He shuddered. Time and time again, all of these thoughts kept raging about in his mind as he looked at the moon and stars above him and tried to stay awake. Later that evening, on a bed of straw, he fell asleep dreaming of Maria.

***

The noises of the animals woke him up. The cows were fretting about the pen in an agitated state mooing, while a few of the chickens he could hear squawking, aroused from their deep slumbers. Inching back as far as he could into the corner of the corral, he reached for the gun and brought it up to his shoulder. He could not see anything but the whites of the animals' eyes, which, thankfully, were reflected by the light of the moon in the dark night. With the half-moon, there was enough light to discern movement in the darkness that surrounded the farm. He prayed for his eyesight to adjust so that he could see the beast prior to it discovering him. He had never shot a coyote before and he found his hands shaking and his heart pounding so loud he thought he could hear it. When he thought of his plan during the day, it had seemed so easy, but now that the animal was in his presence, his adrenaline surged through his body, and he began sweating under the straw while straining to see what was happening around him. He was so afraid that he could not stop the gun from shaking, no matter how hard he tried to stay calm. Momentarily, he thought of his poor friend Fidel, and his resolve came rushing back.

At that moment, the beast leaped into the pen and went directly for the sheep. It was the size of a coyote yet almost looked a bit like a hyena. Stepping up onto the railing, he could see that the animal almost had one of the sheep in its mouth, but when the gun trigger clicked, the animal spun around and glared at him with bright red eyes. It charged, and it took everything Jacinto had not to drop the gun and run, which was his first inclination, but he sighted the gun on the red eyes that were quickly closing the gap. The beast was within a few feet when he pulled the trigger. The recoil sent him stumbling off the railing, and he was unceremoniously dropped on his back. With the wind knocked out of him, and in a state of momentary shock, he found himself gasping for breath and making every effort to get up. He wasn't sure if he had hit the animal and if it was still trying to get to him. A cacophony of strange sounds filled the stable. Kids were screaming, cows were bellowing, sheep were bleating, and through it all, a high-pitched shrill sound of death reigned over the madness, resembling the sound a rabbit makes when it is caught and knows it is going to die, but this noise was much deeper and raspier. He didn't know if he had hit the animal and was scared that it was going to attack him if he didn't get up quickly. It probably was only a few seconds before he finally struggled to his feet, but it felt like his entire life flashed before his eyes.

In the moonlight, he saw the animal lying on its side, half of its face torn up from the gunshot wound. It was a hideous-looking creature, and he really didn't know what it was. He stared at the dead animal, trying to make out exactly what it was, still somewhat scared that it might come back to life and jump up and attack him. It had wrinkly, tough skin with yellowish brown fur and a spine that popped up in a curve. It was not like any coyote he had ever seen before, and if it was, it had caught some horrible disease.

A commanding voice called out to him, "Drop your weapon, and put your hands in the air! Turn around very slowly, and back up until you reach the edge of the corral, son."

He spun around in a dream to the intense white glare of a flashlight. He did not know what was happening and put the gun on the ground next to the animal while walking forward until he had reached the edge of the pen. From the shuffling of their boots on the ground, he could tell there was a bunch of men behind him as well. Someone grabbed him from behind, and he felt the cold steel of handcuffs being placed around his wrists.

The local sheriff turned him around and smiled at him with a contemptuous grin as Jacinto stood shaking in front of him.

"Now, why don't you just tell me what you are doing firing a gun at three in the morning, ok sonny?"

Jacinto explained the whole story, about his lamb being killed the day before, how he had tried to stay awake, and how he had killed the horrible beast that had snuck into the corral for another midnight feast. The officer looked a bit perplexed. He sat Jacinto down on the ground, and not long after, his mother, eyes wide with fear, came rushing out of the house with his sister in her arms. The sheriff returned from the pen after looking at the dead animal and had a brief talk with his deputies. That was when he saw Tomas and Tomas' friend Ben smiling at him, their eyes filled with hate. By now, Tomas' father was there as well, and his heart sank into his stomach. Confusion from the rapid spread of events blotted out every coherent thought that he tried to form in his mind. Soon, the sheriff came over to Tomas' father and spoke with him a bit. Then, they all proceeded to go look at the dead animal again. It was quite a sight to see— three policemen and Tomas' father just staring at the carcass on the ground. The sheriff was squatting next to it, his cowboy hat pulled off, hand furiously scratching at his head.

Soon enough, the sheriff came back over to Jacinto and took off the handcuffs and apologized for cuffing him. The sheriff said that he had been told by the two boys that Jacinto had tried to murder them when they had all agreed to fight earlier in the day at school and that he just didn't believe it after seeing the evidence and hearing Jacinto's story. Jacinto excitedly let the sheriff know he had never promised to fight them in the morning and that they had come by his house to do him and his family harm. The sheriff let him know that what he had done was mighty brave and that he thought he just might have killed the legendary Chupacabra, which, rumor had it, was the cause behind many of the nearby ranchers' problems for years. Tomas's father came over and congratulated him for taking care of his family and protecting them at such a young age. He told him how impressed he was with the boy's maturity and let him know that he reminded him of himself when he was young man and had to scrape by in Mexico. By now, the two other boys' smiles had turned into looks of fear. As Jacinto told his mother and sister what had happened, the sheriff and Tomas' father conferred separately away from everyone before coming back over to speak with Jacinto.

"Jacinto, I believe you might just be eligible for a fifteen-thousand-dollar reward that was placed by ranchers for whomever killed the beast that had been killing their livestock all these years. Also, Don Julio has decided to match the reward by way of a scholarship fund so that by the time you finish school, you should have enough money to go to college." Tomas began to protest, but his mother shot him a look that told him to be quiet.

After everyone left, Jacinto told his mother about the past few days at school and what had happened. By the light of the candle in their small kitchen, he could see her big, beaming smile. He had not seen her smile like that since she and papa had been together, back when he was still alive. It dawned on him that she saw papa in him at that moment. They both smiled at each other, and for a change, both of them looked forward to the coming of the dawn as they sat around the breakfast table talking.

The Fortune Teller

With small white-capped waves rushing in toward the shoreline, Charlotte stood looking at the vastness of the Atlantic Ocean, and although she hadn't moved for the past half hour, if someone had asked her how long she had been there, she would not have been able to say. She was looking for something, but it wasn't out across the waterline like she had hoped; no, it lay somewhere deep in her mind. It had been exactly three years since her mother's disappearance and untimely death, and her mind was racing for answers. Furthermore, just a few weeks ago, her father had passed away from cirrhosis, and, when she had been cleaning out her parent's house, she had stumbled upon an old recording that her mother had made with a fortune teller, of all people. She was bothered by what she had heard from the recording and had decided to try and locate this mysterious fortune teller.

The salty spray, combined with the briny smell that emanated across the beach, triggered a multitude of feelings, ranging from happy memories from her childhood, to feelings of loss and grief. She had lost her mother to the sea, and now, her father was gone too. The loss of her mother still stung, the victim of a boating accident exactly three years ago. She didn't have much empathy for her father, though, not the same way as her mother because he had been absent in her life for as long as she could remember.

Her mother and father had been married for over twenty years in name, but he had secretly wed the whiskey bottle behind her back and never had any room for love or affection. He had treated her mother horribly, and she was happy when the time came to leave the house for college. That had been three years ago as well. She could still remember the phone call that had pulled her out of her astronomy class. It all seemed like a dreadful dream. Her mother had gone missing twenty miles from the shores of Long Island, around Montauk, on a short one-day excursion. It was surreal—her mother had never even been on a boat before as far as she knew. She was a librarian with regular routines, including nightly dinners, the laundry, and cleaning up after her abusive spouse. A fresh spray from the ocean salted her face and surprised and shocked her out of her thoughts, so she decided to glance down at her watch. It was nine o'clock: time for the Coney Island fortune teller to open her shop. She had already tried three other fortune tellers on the island with no luck, but the last fortune teller she had visited had thought for sure she recognized the voice of Esmerelda Chavez on that recording.

Swaying a bit with the wind, she turned her back on the ocean and clutched her purse, where the tape recorder lay neatly tucked inside. Slowly, she made her way across the dunes and toward the antiquated amusement park. She didn't know what to expect and was in fact dreading what she might hear or find, although she didn't exactly know why. What else bad could happen to her that had not already happened? Slogging her way up the dunes in her flats, she knew what it was that was bothering her. There were so many unanswered questions about her mother's tragic ending, and she was hoping, beyond all hope, that she would get some questions answered about the loss of her mother. And there were so many questions. Maybe answers would ease the pain. By now, she had reached the top of the rise of sand that separated the beachfront from the amusement park area, and she stopped at a bench to take off her shoes, emptying them of the sand that had pushed inside. She was stalling the inevitable.

She viewed the Ferris wheel, the octopus ride, the treasure house, and all the booths that soon would be brimming with kids trying to win prizes. At the far end of the boardwalk was the small entrance to Esmerelda's hut. Breathing in deeply, she marched toward the unknown. Upon her arrival, Charlotte quickly noticed that no one was there to greet her.

After a few moments, summoning up what little bit of courage she had, she gathered herself and called out a bit meekly, "Hello, is anybody here?"

Instantly, she heard some rustling from behind the curtain. Then, a small, weathered, deeply wrinkled face the color of mocha appeared from between where the two curtains had come together. And although the face had surely seen thirty thousand suns, the small green eyes embedded within dazzled as if they were from a newborn child.

The fortune teller smiled with a warmth that immediately relaxed her. "Hello my child. Can I help you?" Without replying, save for a nod of the head, Charlotte was ushered inside the fortune teller's hut and given a seat.

Upon her entrance into the dark room behind the curtains, she noticed a small round table at the center of the room with a crystal ball perched directly in the center. Before she knew it, her spine was tingling, her mind was whirring, and the distinct feeling of getting goosebumps came to her arms. The lighting in the room consisted of a few long candles that stood upright on small tables on both sides of the room, and behind them, two large mirrors caught the light. The faint smell of jasmine smoke permeated the air. The room was neither dark nor light, much like the onset of twilight, when things are just visible, albeit in an altered state.

"Now dear, how can I help you? Do you want your fortune read?'

"Well, um maybe. I have a problem, well no, maybe not a problem, but an issue. I think? I believe my mother came here a few years ago, and you told her fortune. In fact, by the sound of the tape recording I ha–a–a–ve . . ." She paused and cleared her throat. "I can almost with full certainty say that you read her fortune by the sound of your voice. The problem is that she died three years ago. And while I was cleaning her house out over the past two weeks, I found this, um, er . . . recording, and I don't know what to think about it and was wondering if you could help me understand it?"

At this, Esmerelda straightened a bit in her chair and pushed her face across the table, peering at her from behind the crystal ball. After a few moments of silence, a faint grin spread across her old, creased face.

"Yes, you look familiar my child . . . you must be the daughter of Desiree. I remember your mother, a kind woman with a good heart. I am so sorry to hear that she passed away. That is very tragic. If I can be so blunt to ask, how did this happen?"

Charlotte noticed that as she spoke, she seemed a bit puzzled and truly concerned about the plight of her mother. Not having someone to confide in for years, she heard herself telling the whole story about the fateful day her mother left, how she had grabbed Charlotte's hands prior to leaving and told her to never to worry about her, and that she loved her. The weird thing was that she had never had any previous inclinations to go out deep sea fishing, but for weeks had talked about it as though it would be something fun and different and that she was really looking forward to it. She had been the only one, out of her entire office, lucky enough to win a ticket to go on a deep sea fishing excursion.

On the day of the excursion, the weather was sunny but with strong gusting winds. Not concerned in the slightest, she had arrived at Montauk at seven in the morning for the chartered fishing trip. By noon, according to the Coast Guard, the boat would have been thirty miles from shore, out over deep water far in the Atlantic Ocean. That was when the weather changed for the worse, and the barometer suddenly dipped. By two in the afternoon, a faint distress signal had been captured over a police radio. Twenty-foot high swells were rolling across the ocean. Later the next day, multiple pieces of the boat were found strewn across the sea, some washing up on the shore. This was the only proof needed to call off the search. Ironically, the only two on board were her mother and the captain. The news media had descended upon the family like a pack of barracuda in a feeding frenzy, only to leave them alone just as quickly after the bones of their humble and tragic lives were picked clean and the news story had run its course. Her life had been shattered forever, but her father, although stuck by the inconvenience of making his own dinner, didn't appear to change one iota, other than the amount of whiskey he consumed, which steadily increased over time. She had been glad not to have to be around him and had found refuge at college. And now he was dead as well.

At this piece of information, Esmerelda's eyes, which had grown sullen and cloudy, suddenly flickered with light, and she asked to hear the recording of her fortune telling from years ago. The recording began.

You feel as if your life is a prison with a golden sparrow that feeds from you. It is but your one true love in this world, and it is going away as well. The prison walls are closing in on you, but I foresee that these walls are going to crumble away in front of your very eyes. The sea will take you to the other side of life. This escape is possible, and through it, you will find true happiness. Although the sorrow of the loss of your sparrow will ring hollow in your heart, it too shall pass knowing that you have provided what is necessary for it to fly unhindered upon its own destiny. The seas may be rough at first, but if you follow your heart, in the end, you shall overcome

*and find true happiness, and even the sparrow that you
have cut free will come home to roost upon your shores.
Fortune, which has been denied you for many years, will
smile upon your face if you pray to the God of Neptune.*

"Hmm . . . that is a very curious fortune, indeed, that
I gave your mother. I shall have to think about this. Did
your mother leave you anything when she died? Any
notes or papers or trinkets or jewelry?"

"Well she made me the beneficiary of her life insurance policy, which has kept me in college. My father was
furious when he found out that she had somehow gotten
him to sign off on the policy when he was in one of his
drunken stupors, but there was nothing he could do about
it. Other than that, she didn't leave me anything else that
I know of. I mean, don't get me wrong, she ultimately
provided for me, but how did you know it was going to
occur by her being killed in a freak accident at sea?"

"Think hard if she left you anything else," Esmerelda
said in a controlling voice as she waved her hand over
the crystal ball, bringing up a wave of purple flame from
deep inside.

Charlotte began digging within her purse. From it,
she produced a piece of paper that she found next to the
recording when she had been searching in the attic. She
pushed it across the table to where the old woman sat.
On it was scrawled an unintelligible message. Scrolled

in all small letters was the following: "Veritas eventually rewarded, and child returned under Zapata."

"I really don't know what to make of it. First, it has three different languages on the note, English, Spanish, and Latin. Then, it makes a reference to a child returned under a shoe? It is all in lower case, except the words 'Veritas' and 'Zapata,' and my mother was the best at English grammar and rules, being that she was a librarian. None of it makes much sense to me at all."

For more than a minute, the old woman sat there thinking, her head slightly tilted downward as if gazing into the crystal ball. Not wanting to interrupt her train of thought, Charlotte wondered if she hadn't been a fool for coming here. She waited for Esmerelda to speak. The old woman turned and fumbled in a drawer behind her and then turned with her fiery jade-colored green cat's eyes lovingly staring at her.

"My dear is this your mother?," she said as she produced a polaroid picture of her mom and a handsome Spanish-looking man both smiling on the deck of the charter boat, the very boat that they had both been killed on that fateful day.

Gasping back the tears, she could not believe it. They both looked so happy—almost too happy—as if they were in love, with his arm slung around her shoulders.

Esmerelda, in a soft voice, began to speak, "By now, my dear, you are old enough to be told the truth. I have been waiting for you. Your mother was frightfully unhappy in her marriage, as you probably surmised, and when you left home to go to college, things only got darker for her. You were her little sparrow, and the prison was her home that she lived in with your father. She met a man who loved her, the one you see in the picture, but she had no way to leave your father and still afford to send you to college. She even confided in me that she had contemplated suicide, but the insurance company would not pay off if that occurred, and so the two of them devised a plan. And I was part of it.

She paused for a moment, that fire raging in her eyes. "I recorded the message so that when your ill father passed away and you found the recording cleaning out the house, you would come looking for me. The note is purposefully vague, but I believe if you read the message again, you might just find your mother's whereabouts. Try the first letter from each word, and then use the last word to find her (Veritas eventually rewarded, and child returned under Zapata). The only hard part of her plan was not being able to tell you, for obvious reasons. Now child, I think you might want to start making plans to travel to Zapata Street in Veracruz Mexico. And do give her my warmest regards. Always remember, my dear, that sometimes one's good fortune must be created by oneself, albeit with a little help from a fortune teller."

Alfred the Mule

Johnny awoke and found himself staring at the most beautiful creature he had ever seen. It had four legs, a head much like a donkey's, and a shiny sleek coat of all different colors of white, cream, black, burnt orange, tan, and light yellow construed in a piebald fashion. The colors mixed and blended together to form the most pleasant sight he could think of. After looking at this magnificent animal for a few minutes, Johnny began to realize he did not recognize where he was. It seemed an amazing place. As far as he could see, he was surrounded by sand the color of the sun while a bright blue cobalt sky stretched seemingly forever. In the pale light of the dawn, he could still see the bright twinkling stars and the last vestiges of the moon, faint as it was. Gently, the breeze caused him to look to his left. In front of his eyes was the most wonderfully lush oasis he had ever seen. Peppermint-colored water spread out before his eyes, and it was surrounded by all types of tropical bushes and towering palm trees. There were fig trees, date palms, and large banana plants with wide open leaves hanging low from the heavy fruit dripping from their boughs. He could not have dreamed of a more beautiful and serene place. A feeling of warmth and happiness spread though his body and filled him with an unbelievable sense of calm. Just then, the creature he had initially been staring at got up on all four legs, meandered over to the oasis, and began to drink its fill of water from the small pond.

He was not sure what to make of this strange and wondrous animal, and speaking to himself, he asked out loud, "What are you?"

Turning its head to him without turning its body, the animal, much to Johnny's surprise, answered him, "I am a mule of God, of course."

Johnny was astonished that the creature spoke to him. And when the shock dropped away, he managed to ask, "What is a mule of God?"

"I am not sure what you mean," the animal replied.

"Where do you come from? What do you do, and how can you talk like a human?"

"I am not sure of the answers to your questions, but I can tell you that I come from far away, and I only answer truthfully to any questions asked of me. As for how I can talk to you, well that is a trait of a mule, and I can sense your feelings and thoughts just as if they were my own. And it seems to me as if you feel a little lost, not only as to where you are from, but also as to where you are going in life. Furthermore, I can sense your heart is good."

Johnny liked what the animal said because it was true and reassuring that something understood him.

"How did you get here?" Johnny asked.

"I have always been here. What you need to ask is how did you get here?"

"Oh, well I am a bit confused about everything right now, but at least I should know your name," answered Johnny.

"My name is Alfred, and I am a mule beholden to God. I believe I can help you."

"How can you help me?" asked Johnny.

"I can read your mind and help you with your thoughts and wishes. My only mission in life is to help people and animals with their problems. That is what a mule in my position does. I am here to help. It is my purpose in life, and I am unable to do anyone any harm."

"Why that is incredible!" exclaimed Johnny. "You are telling me that your only purpose in life is to help people?"

"Not only people, but every living thing that exists. My purpose is to bring peace and love to all sentient beings and create harmony out of chaos."

Johnny was dumbfounded. How could he be in a strange place with a talking animal whose only goal in life was to help others? This must be a dream. But he could smell the scent of coconuts and figs, the ripe bananas on the trees, hear the sounds of the chirping birds, and feel the moisture over his skin as the breeze lightly blew over the oasis. This was very real.

At that moment, Alfred brushed up against him, and he felt the soft touch of the creature's fur, so exquisite it reminded him of his favorite blanket from his childhood. Somehow, his memories raced back to when he was a child, with warm and comforting thoughts of his mother snuggling him, and his father tickling him. Life was never as good as it was back then. His mind flashed back to many of his fondest memories from long ago, and unbeknownst to him, he lost track of the time and his friend Alfred. Soon, shadows began to cross his face, and he realized that Alfred had wandered over to the oasis and had laid down for a nap. He didn't know for how long he had been daydreaming, but it must have been for a few hours based upon the sun in the sky.

"I am sorry Alfred, but I became lost in thought and completely forgot about what we were talking about," Johnny said as he approached the oasis.

"Did you forget?" Alfred asked questioningly.

"I am not sure?" he replied in a confused and concerned manner.

"You really did not do anything but gain a channel into your subconscious, one looking into your childhood. I put you there for your own benefit. It seemed to me that you needed to reconnect with your past because you were having feelings of loss and confusion concerning the present."

"What do you mean? Did you cause this?" exclaimed Johnny with much excitement and surprise.

"Yes, of course I did. How else could you gather your thoughts to rationalize your feelings of happiness and yet trepidation. You are in a new environment, and it was necessary to not only soothe your psyche, but to give you the reassurance of your youth by flashing back to comforting times from the past. It is simple really."

"How did you do that?"

"Like I said before, I can read your thoughts. Upon reading your concerns, I gathered your fears together and made sure you were able to reconstruct your ego, your own self-worth in other words, with gentle and good memories from your past. I did this when I brushed up against you. Do you remember?"

"You mean you caused my memories by touching me?"

"Yes," replied Alfred.

"But how?"

"I am a mule of God."

"I have never heard of anything in my life that can do what you do. It seems to me to be impossible and yet you are next to me?"

"Impossible, no, not really. Just improbable according to your laws and conceptions of the universe, but I will let you know it is possible, and it has happened! You are the living truth."

"Can I learn how to do this?" asked Johnny.

Alfred let out a long sigh, and it seemed his whole thought, mind, and body had exhaled with just that very simple motion. It was a deep, long sigh, and he replied very cautiously and carefully, "Yes, maybe you can. One has to learn much about themselves to be aware of their own actions. A certain level of introspection of oneself has to be attained."

Upon uttering those words, the mule nodded to him, turned its back, and curled up in a ball. It was more than evident the mule was ready to sleep. Taking his cue, Johnny lay next to the mule, and soon, both of them were fast asleep. And even though the desert became quite cold that night, he was warmed by the animal that had been so kind to him, and he felt as though he was floating on clouds with not a care in the world.

***

When Johnny awoke in the morning, Alfred was gone. With a terrible fear that he had lost his friend, he began searching the area frantically. After a few minutes, he spotted the mule soaking in the sun and munching some dates from a low-hanging fruit tree.

"Good morning Johnny. How did you sleep?" asked Alfred.

"I think it was the best sleep I ever had. I thought I had lost you this morning when I did not see you and was upset to think that maybe I would never see you again."

The mule lowered its head a bit and looked at Johnny very seriously. "I want to tell you a secret. I will actually never leave you your whole life as long as you believe in doing the right thing and keep your actions and thoughts admirable to those around you. Remember, I am the mule of God."

Johnny wanted to believe Alfred, but it was hard to imagine the mule always being around him, just by doing the right things in his life. This was very hard for him to understand, and he felt confused.

"If you are not with me, then how can you say you are actually with me? This sounds like a bit of trickery," Johnny said with an uncertain look.

"You are young and have much to learn about physically being with someone and the difference between being spiritually connected to someone. If I am with you in your mind, then I am with you whether or not I am actually in your presence," Alfred replied.

There was a silence of understanding among them that day while they played and ate the lush fruits of the oasis. Life was very good for the both of them. Soon, one day turned into a week and then, soon after, a month of wonderful conversations, exploration, and play. On one particularly bright day with the orange sun high above them, Johnny happened to see smoke rising from very far off in the distance, and he became curious, wanting to know what was causing it. He felt the need to travel to the smoke and find out who was there, but Alfred warned him that the world could be a very cruel place, especially to a young man such as himself. Throughout the day, his curiosity kept increasing as the hours slipped by, and by nightfall, he had decided that the next day he would go and find out for himself who and what was making the smoke.

In the morning, before Alfred awoke, Johnny quietly packed a few things to travel with, mostly fruits, figs, dates, and a few coconuts. Looking out along the horizon, he could still see the wisps of smoke rising from the west. It was not that he had been unhappy at the oasis. On the contrary, he was filled with wonder and admiration for the mule and all of the special ways of looking at the ways of the world Alfred had taught him. For this, he was very happy, but his sense of adventure had helped to make his decision to travel across the desert and explore the world around him.

With a spring in his step, he began the journey. Within just a few hours, he began to feel tired and wondered if he had not made a mistake. He thought of what Alfred must be doing and thinking because he had left without saying goodbye or even giving a thanks for the magical days spent at the oasis. He felt a bit ashamed of this but had not wanted to listen to the reasoning of the mule or any of his warnings of possible trouble in a land so far away. He was consumed with wanderlust. He was old enough to make his own decisions and did not want any meddling from someone so learned and wise. As he continued to trudge through the sand, he began to feel some resentment in his heart toward Alfred, although for no good earthly reason. The traveling was much harder than he had thought. The sun, his friend at the oasis, was now his mortal enemy. It beat down upon him relentlessly, and he cursed it for its power and oppressive heat. Why hadn't Alfred mentioned this? But he knew that was silly because everyone knew walking in the desert was fraught with many perilous hazards. He knew he was angry at himself for not listening to the warnings that had been given to him.

At midday, he decided to rest underneath the branches of a dead tree, which gave him some shelter from the heat. After sweating profusely for hours, his body had stopped sweating and his stomach was in knots. He knew this to be an ominous sign. He ate slowly, thinking of all the good times he had at the oasis. When he looked in the distance toward the smoke, he knew he was still many miles away and decided it was probably better if he traveled at night. After eating and drinking most of his meager supply of food and coconut milk, he lay down and took a nap.

***

When he awoke much later, he could hear the sound of the desert wind howling, crying out like the sound of a lost animal in the night, and he shuddered to himself, thinking about the long lonely journey in front of him. He ate the last of his food and began to walk in the direction of the smoke, which was still visible against the night sky. All night, he struggled through the sand, biting wind, and bitter cold. By morning, he was staring at the walls of a huge fort that rose high above the ground. From behind the walls, he could smell the scent of meat cooking.

In an instant, he found himself surrounded by four guards with spears pointed at him. Each of them had long curved swords attached to their belts, leather body armor, and helmets of silvery metal perched atop their heads. Smiling at him, malice in their eyes, they shoved him to the ground, bound his hands, and commanded him to walk to the front of the fort where an immense wooden door with iron hinges stood.

"You are our prisoner now," said the largest of the guards, who stood well over six feet high.

"But what have I done?" asked Johnny incredulously.

"It does not matter. You were trespassing outside the gates of the almighty King of the Desert, Modnar the IV, and you shall die like the rest of the slaves and trespassers."

The shock of his death sentence was immediate. He could not talk and felt the weight of a thousand stones attached to his legs; and his heart felt as though it had been dropped off a cliff, like a stone falling from the peak of a canyon into the depths of a chasm. He saw them looking at him, laughing and talking about how pleased their king would be to have a new prisoner. They marched him through the gate and into a huge courtyard, and there he saw the most appalling and macabre sight he had ever witnessed.

In front of him were a dozen men, all tied to stakes, screaming in agony as they were being roasted alive in front of a crowd of townspeople, who were clearly enjoying the ghastly spectacle. He realized then that he was in a truly savage land. At the far end of the courtyard sat the king—draped in a fine red robe and wearing a splendid crown of gold—looking very pleased with himself. They marched him along to the corner of the courtyard, where they untied his hands and threw him inside a prison cell. Looking around in the darkness of the cell, he could see men of all ages sitting against the walls peering at him, pained expressions etched on their faces. The filth on their skin, their emaciated bodies, and hollow piercing stares let him know that he was doomed to the same fate as the men in the courtyard. Why had he not listened to Alfred the mule?

He looked around his new surroundings, seeing that he was in a simple square cell with the prison bars facing the courtyard. The ground was hard packed dirt with some straw strewn around for the comfort of the prisoners. In all, he counted a total of five other men in the prison, all obviously malnourished and the color of white parchment from a lack of sun. It seemed to him that he was the youngest of all of them. Within a few minutes, they began to ask him questions about how he came to be with them and why he was wandering the desert alone. He told them his story. He went into detail about how the mule was able to read his mind and how the amazing animal could talk. Then, he let them know that even though he had been warned about leaving and traveling to the strange land, he had decided to cross the desert anyway only to find himself here.

After hearing his story, the other prisoners laughed and looked at him in a very funny way. Soon, much to his dismay, he was labeled "crazy with heatstroke since he talked to animals," and they all had a good time at his expense. Johnny felt very depressed. He admitted to himself that his adventure was not believable, and yet it was true! Despite their laughter and scorn, he wanted to know when they were to die. The simple pleasure of teasing him was extinguished when he asked when they were to receive their collective death sentence.

One of the taller prisoners, who had a long beard and red hair, spoke with a strong voice which settled them all down, "Tomorrow, we play soccer against the guards. Whomever loses is subject to the punishment their opponent chooses. The last group of prisoners angered the guards by daring to score a goal, and they had them burned at the stake. These people are very ruthless and without feeling."

"Then we have a chance at freedom if we win!" exclaimed Johnny.

"If you call playing against the king's professional team a chance, then you are crazier then we first thought. They train every day, eat the best food, and sleep in the finest beds. Meanwhile, we are given an hour to get ready for the game, eat scraps and gruel, sleep on the hard ground, and know nothing of playing soccer together. The last team lost twenty to one."

The hope that had risen within Johnny just a few seconds prior soon vanished. Through the bars, he viewed the guards practicing with exquisite skill, speed, and strength as they kicked the ball around the field. Then, he looked around the cell and saw a bunch of tired, forlorn, and emaciated prisoners. His stomach began to hurt from hunger even though it had only been a few days since he had left the oasis. He could not think of anything to do. Soon, he sat down and began to think of the mule and the wonderful times they had together. He found himself praying that he was here with him. Between his prayers, lack of food, and worries about the next day's soccer match, he found himself drifting off to sleep.

He awoke to the sound of the cell door opening and clanging shut. In the dark, he could barely see anything, except for a few precious rays of moonlight that filtered through the bars. Incredibly, there stood the mule! All of the prisoners stared in amazement at the strange and beautiful creature.

The guard yelled at them, "Here you go. This is the last member of your soccer team. I found it wandering around the fort walls, and since it resembles an ass of some sorts, I thought it fitting to put it in with you." The guard bellowed with laughter at his own joke.

In the dark, the mule replied to the guard, "Sometimes, maybe, the ass is the one who does the talking and does not even know it."

At this, everybody laughed at the guard, and he demanded to know who had dared speak to him, but no one answered him as they continued laughing. He left grumbling to himself and letting them know under his breath that tomorrow would be their last day on earth.

After the laughter died down, it became very quiet since they all realized that it was the animal that had spoken, and that Johnny had been telling the truth.

Johnny approached Alfred and spoke, "I am so glad to see you, and I am sorry for leaving you so abruptly. Now, though, I am very sorry. I have sealed your fate as well. We are all sentenced to die tomorrow after we play soccer against the guards."

"Who is to say we are going to lose?" replied Alfred with a twinkle in his eye.

"Nobody has ever beaten them, and we are but a hungry bunch of prisoners," said one of the younger prisoners.

"The most important thing is to have faith and not give up. What everyone needs is a good meal and some sleep. I will take care of that," replied Alfred.

Walking over to the door of the prison cell, Alfred turned around, and with a kick from one of its powerful back legs, busted the lock. The door swung open. The mule turned toward them and let them know he would be back in a minute. A few minutes, later Alfred returned with saddle bags bulging with food and drink. Ravenously, the prisoners opened the saddle bags. They found a roast turkey and ham, grapes, and assorted cheeses and some bottles of red wine. Alfred heartily laughed and let them know that the king would probably begin to wonder how his evening meal had disappeared. Alfred said that he had snuck into the kitchen, and when the staff had gone to serve refreshments, he had filled the saddle bags with food. The famished prisoners voraciously feasted upon the ham and turkey, drank of the red wine, and laughed about the king's misfortune and their good luck to have met Alfred. That evening, for the first time in months, they talked and laughed and enjoyed a good meal. Their bellies were full of food, and they knew they would sleep well. It was a shame, they said, that even though they were free of the cell, they still could not get past the front gates of the fort, or otherwise they would have attempted to escape that night. As the evening wound down, Alfred brushed up against each one of them and transported each to special place within their own consciousness. They slept like rocks.

***

In the morning, the prisoners were let out of the cell and led to the center of the city where the amphitheater awaited. Within this city-like fortress, hidden in the eastern portion of the Dwengili desert, the Kingdom of Modnar the IV was witness to a monthly slaughtering of other peoples from beyond the country's borders. Alfred appeared upbeat, but his team members were acting as though they had already been sentenced to death. As each of them entered the field of play, he touched them and congratulated them for having the courage to face death. They looked at him with strange faces and looks of astonishment.

"Hey, what are you doing," asked one of the prisoners. "Are you trying to give me rabies?"

Alfred laughed.

"Have you given up on us already, you crazy mule?" asked another one of them.

Alfred laughed again. The men could sense his courage and unflappable spirit. It was contagious.

"No, you should be fine today," Alfred replied.

The words of encouragement were music to the ears of a bunch of tired and beaten men. Each of them received a personal message and words of encouragement as they passed by him, feeling the mule's strength and conviction of spirit.

After the horns and long thin trumpets blew to signal the start of the game, the crowd became quiet with anticipation. To begin the game, the guards expertly took the ball down the field, showing off their passing skills. From the center of the field, the ball went to the right, and immediately, the prisoners were on their heels, attempting to catch up and play defense. Alfred had elected himself to be the goaltender. Adeptly, the guards moved the ball all the way down to the prisoner's goal, and when one of the guards kicked the ball toward the net with a slicing kick, the crowd rose up in their seats expecting a goal. Then, with the ball slicing toward the net, another guard used his head to redirect the ball toward the upper corner. As the referee got ready to sound the whistle, he stopped. Within a split second, much faster than many in the stands could see or that many on the field of play could believe, the ball was scooped up by Alfred and booted down the field all the way to the opposing goaltender. An awed hush settled over the crowd. It all happened so fast that it did not seem possible. In utter amazement, the guards and prisoners stared at Alfred, all a bit stupefied by what they had just witnessed.

Alfred stretched a bit and yawned and took a long drink, and after, he said to the guards, "Better luck next time, eh boys?"

After getting over their initial shock, the guards became very angry. This was supposed to be an easy game in which they scored at will against the helpless prisoners, thereby receiving accolades from the crowd and gifts from the king. Determined to score, they again drove the ball down the field of play and marched almost directly up to the goalie, but again, the same thing happened. Alfred was blindingly fast and was seemingly having a good time stopping them from scoring. In fact, he was immensely enjoying himself, and the crowd could sense the frustration from the guards. Every time the ball got remotely close to crossing the goal line, Alfred would grab and kick it the length of the field so that the guards would have to go chase it down and bring it back the full length of the field. This happened over and over again. At halftime, it was a scoreless game.

With less than a few minutes to go, it was still a scoreless affair. By this time, the crowd was laughing at the guards and cheering on the prisoners, much to the dismay of the king and the other team. They laughed and screamed with delight when Alfred effortlessly stopped all of their best shots. Whether by corner kick, penalty kick, crossing route, or header, they were denied. As the referee signaled that only one minute remained in the match, they attempted one more time to score. This time, they took a long kick from the corner and placed it right in front of the goalie, but this time, they did not shoot it. Instead, the guard in the center swiftly passed it to another guard on his right, which left Alfred out of position. With a quick driving kick, the ball soared toward the net. But alas, once again, it was stopped by Alfred, who had a smile on his face.

"Nice try that time, eh boys?"

And with that, Alfred kicked the ball halfway down the field and sprinted after it. Leaving his own goal empty, he got to the ball first and drove the rest of the length of the field. Everyone on the field was running after him, but nobody could catch him. As the other goalie watched with a mixture of fear and hate, Alfred ran directly at him and booted the ball as hard as he could. The mule directed the ball toward the top right corner of the net. The goaltender's look of determined hate turned into a look of astonishment and fear. The ball was flying directly into the top corner of the net, a place virtually impossible for the goalie to reach. The goalie leaped for the ball, but it passed by his fingertips and dropped into the back of the net. Almost immediately, the whistle sounded three times, indicating the end of the game.

The crowds were delirious. Horns were blowing, whistles sounding, all while people were yelling and jumping into each other's arms, screaming with joy. They had never seen such a soccer match in their whole lives. The prisoners hoisted Alfred on their shoulders and shouted and jumped for joy. Some of them sobbed, while others could not stop running around the field in their excitement. As for the guards, many of them sat down on the field in shock, while others walked around aimlessly, not believing what had just happened.

After a few minutes, the crowd began to quiet down. The king, although very angry at his guards' poor play, pronounced that the prisoners were free to go and that he would grant them one wish as well. As for the losing soccer team, he turned to them and, with a smirking look of disdain, ordered that all of them be arrested. He pronounced the guards would be put to death. For the king, it was such a mighty insult to see his guards beaten that in his anger and shame at their pitiful showing on the field, wanted to show the people that he was still in control even if they weren't.

The guards were mortified by their death sentence. A few of them began weeping. Precisely at this moment, in a loud and clear voice, Johnny spoke to the king.

With all of the prisoners and Alfred behind him, Johnny asked for the one wish that had been granted to them by their victory. The king, pleased with himself for thinking of such a powerful way to show who made the laws in the land, quickly asked what the prisoners wanted.

John paused and then said, "As we will be leaving your land this evening and never again wish to be in such a cruel tyrannical place as this, we merely ask that for our one wish, you grant clemency for the guards."

And with that, the crowds went crazy to the point of it feeling like a volcano had erupted within the stadium. Pandemonium had broken out in the kingdom. All of the guards were hugging each other, the guard's families were crying, the horns were blaring, and the king, depleted of all his strength and power, slumped into his throne, thoroughly beaten.

As the townspeople continued to celebrate, the prisoners made their way out of the gates of the fortress and into the freedom of the desert. Johnny looked at Alfred and smiled as Alfred smiled back at him, letting him know that he knew what Johnny was thinking. Johnny had learned many things these past few months, and forgiveness was one of them. As the sun began to set, they walked toward it, setting off in the direction of the oasis, and did not bother to look back at the Kingdom of Modnar IV.

It seemed impossible to most of them that they were walking free, heading toward a new life, when only a day prior, they had all been condemned to die. And it was all because of Alfred the mule of God. Their hearts were alive and singing with joy and love, and each of them had a new-found respect for the power of faith. They laughed and spoke reverently of the mule of God. That is, until they looked around and noticed the mule was gone! Panic stricken, some of them called out his name in vain, but no answer came back. Johnny, as surprised as the rest of them, merely smiled to himself. Johnny nodded to himself. What better an animal than a mule, who is made to carry many of the burdens of man upon his back every day, to carry the word of God and love to his children on earth?

"He is still with us, my friends, and he will always be with us as long as we have hope in God and do the right things and act accordingly with His wishes. I remember that is what he told me, so we must have faith that he is always around us," Johnny said.

And as they looked up into the sky, the very first star of the night appeared above the horizon, seemingly right above the oasis, as if Alfred was once again guiding them in their quest for salvation.

The Lost Explorers

Rapidly accelerating, the spaceship zipped up to the red giant known as Prometheus Four, a sun nestled within the gamma quadrant. The helmsman could see the temperature gauge approaching ten thousand degrees. The maximum temperature sustainable by the ship, which measured less than fifty feet in length, was just below seventeen thousand degrees and would be reached within the next few minutes. At one precise moment, they would be flung like a rock from a slingshot and boomeranged out into space using the immense gravitational pull of the red giant. Even traveling at a quarter of the speed of light, it would take them another six months to reach their destination.

The helmsman began the countdown to firing up the afterburner engines, and then with a flick of his long, cerulean-colored finger, switched them on. Instantly, the ship sped around the backside of the giant sun and raced away into space toward its exploratory mission. Some sixty-two years prior, one of their ships had sent a distress call and was never heard from again. As historical researchers and explorers, they found themselves settling into their individual chambers for a sleep that would consume them for the next six months. Upon their arrival, they would awaken from their hibernation and begin their research into the mystery of their comrades' ill-fated mission.

***

As the sensors began chiming within the spacecraft alerting them to the small planet below, the crew readied themselves for the upcoming mission. Extra amounts of helium and oxygen were pumped into the cabin to keep them fully alert and prepared to deal with any possible signs of danger from the unknown world. The readings that they were getting from the planet indicated that it was teaming with millions of different species of organisms and that over two-thirds of the planet was covered with water. Further sensory readings revealed that multiple satellites were in orbit around the planet, thus confirming their initial hypothesis that intelligent life was present.

Stationing themselves just outside of the gravitational pull of the planet, they began to pull data from the planet by opening all of the ship's incoming communication channels. The three-man crew filtered through the videos and incoming transmissions using a universal language modulator. This not only got them the information they needed in a version they could understand, but also in a condensed format, saving them time. For the next twelve hours, they studied the inhabitants. The level of scientific knowledge of the different animals was studied and categorized. The laws and customs of the dominant primary species were also scrutinized. Further study was performed on the amount of care and compassion shown to the weakest members of this species, as well as to the treatment of other species.

The cursory analysis was disturbing. The dominant species of the planet was an extremely war-happy animal that had little or no compassion for either members of its own species and even less so for the other creatures that inhabited their planet. Full-scale wars had been fought throughout the history of the planet, killing billions of them. Slavery was endemic to many parts of their world, and the ruling classes used a tool known as "specie or money" to separate themselves from the masses of the working classes. The police and law systems were utilized to keep this separation intact without any regard to justice. Animals across the planet were systematically killed either for pleasure or to keep them away from food crops, which could then be sold for money. In other cases, other life forms were simply in the way of what the dominant species described as "progress" and went extinct because of the destruction of their habitat. Finally, the predominant species of the planet seemed to have an innate fixation on how another one of their kind looked or what color their skin was, which in turn caused them to randomly lash out and kill each other.

Weapons were built to indiscriminately kill thousands at a time, and everything from nuclear bombs to poison gases was employed to gain possession and control of the planet's natural resources.

In a review of the dominant species' technological accomplishments, it was clearly astounding what had transpired over the past one hundred years. Mass farming techniques yielded an abundance of food compared with the previous small subsistence farms that had dominated the planet for thousands of years. Computer and robotic technology had been invented within the past fifty years and had yielded the first foray off of the planet and into the realm of space exploration. The fields of medicine, biology, and animal husbandry had achieved more in the past one hundred years than in the preceding five thousand years, but the uses of this knowledge were not always for the betterment of the planet. Mass farming had come with mass deforestation and, coupled with the use of pesticides, was rapidly poisoning the fresh water sources of the planet. Extra supplies of food were not delivered to the starving members of the world but rather left to rot in silos. The technological revolution had not gone to benefit the individual members of the species just to replace them and marginalize their existence. Animals were now bred in captivity, living their lives in deplorable conditions, mostly in cramped filthy quarters while being force fed antibiotics inserted within their food so that they could be sold for more money. With each advance in technology, the common thread was a lust for money and a complete separation from any form of compassion for any living thing.

The three crew members decided it was a very hostile planet and realized that they must be extremely cautious in the search for their missing comrades. They switched on a sweeper to look for high concentrations of two of their base metals found within their ships made sixty years prior and began a full-scale search of the planet. Within just a few minutes, they located a high concentration of these two metals. As night fell, they descended into an arid land and could see that it was cordoned off from the surrounding areas by fences. There were multiple structures inside of this enclosed area. Noiselessly, they landed and began their search for answers.

Zeroing in on the concentrations of the rare elements brought them to a deserted area. The instruments indicated that very small amounts of debris were spread out over a wide radius, most likely from the crash of the ship over sixty years ago. It occurred to them that the dominant species of the planet had more than likely already examined the area and taken away any remnants of the ship. Furthermore, they would probably not find any remains of their comrades. Had they survived the crash and were somehow still alive? It seemed an extremely remote possibility that they could have survived on the planet with such a warring species dominating the landscape. Flicking on a medical scanner, they blasted out a stream of deionized protons in all directions to see if they could locate the bodies. What happened next astounded all three of them. Clearly and distinctly, the scanner began clicking. Excitedly, all three of them looked at the instrument. There were indications that one of their comrades had survived and was located below one of the large buildings directly in front of them.

Back at the ship, they began formulating a plan to rescue their comrade. Quietly, they moved out of the ship and commenced the rescue mission. Cloaked in protective suits, and armed with stun guns, tranquilizers, and sleeping gas canisters, they easily entered the facility after disabling a few of the creatures at the entranceways. Making their way through the labyrinth of hallways within the cavernous building, the medical sensor kept clicking faster and faster, alerting them to their comrade's presence. After disabling a few more guards at an entrance to an elevator, they descended to the lowest level, finding themselves over three hundred feet beneath the surface of the planet. The medical sensor clicked continuously now. They knew they were close. The doors to the elevator opened to reveal a circular room with a table situated directly in the center. On the table lay the old explorer, their comrade, with tubes sticking out of his body in all directions. He was strapped to the table with restraints on both of his arms and legs and appeared to be in a comatose, almost lifeless, state although his vital signs from the medical sensor indicated he was alive. Slowly, he opened his eyes, turning toward them. The tears that streamed from the sides of his eyes and down his cheeks let them know he had recognized them. They struggled with the straps, attempting to release him. With each disconnection of a tube running into his body or strap cut, an audible, clanging alarm went off. Once unstrapped and unhooked, the leader of the crew shouldered him onto his back and carried him to the elevator. Swiftly, they made their way out of the facility and back to the ship, but not before a few more of the creatures had to be disabled. It took them less than an hour to retrieve their comrade. Furthermore, and most importantly, they had not permanently harmed any of the species that were guarding him. This was part of their code when interacting with beings from other planets.

What they learned from the withered explorer made them angry and sad. What had started as an exploratory mission to find other sentient beings in the universe had turned into a barbaric story of torture and imprisonment that had continued for over sixty-two years. After both he and another crew member had been taken alive from the crash site, the explorer had watched helplessly as they had dissected his friend, who had been clinging to life, alive. They had learned from the dissection what sustenance was necessary to keep him alive all these years and had pumped that into him with feeding tubes. For decades, they had attempted to communicate with him but did not have the advanced technology needed to make a universal translator. From the remnants of the crashed ship, they had been able to reverse engineer many of the technological advances that had transformed their society over the past fifty years. As for him, he was kept alive and imprisoned on the table with the hope that someday, they could eventually communicate with him. Sadly, after thousands of failed attempts to communicate with him, he was merely kept alive as a specimen to be occasionally looked at by some high-ranking dignitary, like he was some sort of sideshow oddity.

The crew did not need to see anything more on the planet. Their mission was complete. It was startling and disturbing to them to find such a technologically ad-vanced race with such a primitive mindset. Their mis-sions were logged within the memory banks of the ship's computers. Before leaving for the long trip back to their home planet, they decided to take a picture of the facility where they had rescued the old explorer. Into the ship's memory banks went one last piece of data, a snapshot that read: "KEEP OUT RESTRICTED FACILITY AREA 51."

The Lodge

Long before the low fuel light began blinking, I had known I was in trouble. Over a few hundred miles had been put between me and the Mexican border as I drove through windy, cutback roads within the Angeles National Forest. My gas tank kept creeping lower and lower, all without a gas station in sight along the main road that would, eventually I could hope, lead me to the white sands of Alamogordo New Mexico.

And then it happened.

A gas station lay in front of me. Excitedly, I pulled in and could see plastic bags wrapped around the only two pump handles at the gas station. They were out of gas! And I was out of luck. Pulling back on the roadway, I found myself cursing the gas station for not having any gas, feeling extremely tense about my current situation. I had no idea that here in the United States, you could still have places that did not have warning signs that stated how many miles before another gas stop, and I had traveled over two hundred miles! I felt annoyed at New Mexico and myself. And then the remote stretch of road suddenly turned even windier, and I began a long uphill climb into the towering pine, pinon, and juniper trees that controlled the landscape.

The trees seemingly mocked my plight, towering above my puny car like monuments standing tall against the ravages of the human race run amok. Silently emanating their hidden power, they harked back to the days when ancient Apache warriors on horseback ruled this part of the world. That is when my fuel light came on. I cursed them. I cursed them all! With each dinging noise that emanated, my frustration grew, reminding me of what a fool I was for getting this low on gas in a part of the country I was unfamiliar with. For seven more miles, I climbed up into the sparsely populated hills of the forest with my prayers going unanswered. Since the gas station, I had already climbed a few thousand feet. I turned onto the next bend, and there it was, salvation and the answer to my prayers: a gas station. God had been kind to me once again. I made a promise to be more pious and quickly forgot about it.

The Navajo woman behind the register smiled as I told her of my ordeal. She had a pleasant round face that spoke to nothing of her feelings, while her eyes shined like black beads. In between breathing sighs of relief, I asked her where I could get some lunch. She asked me if I was from around here, while assuring her that I was not, a bit indignantly after my little escapade, she smiled and told me I would just have to visit the lodge right across the main highway and up a few streets. It was very famous she told me. Clark Gable and Vivian Leigh had vacationed there. From my upper-middle class Caucasian background, I was impressed and hurried off to my car to go find lunch at this lodge. She smiled at me as I left, without me ever feeling that I knew one thing of what she ever felt toward me, or anything else for that matter.

Driving across the highway and up into the hills, I found it. A magnificent white turn-of-the-century Victorian mansion nestled among the towering pines within the city of Cloudcroft New Mexico. Rain began to fall on the car as I pulled into an empty parking lot. Hurrying to the front door against the blowing, cold wind, I managed to pull the heavy door open against the groans of its hinges.

Stepping inside, I was not disappointed. The walls were painted a regal hunter green, antique Victorian paintings covered the walls, and soft white gaslight emanated across the fine carpets. Passing the front desk, which was oddly empty, I walked up a few stairs and turned to my right, staring into a lounge area crowded with empty round tables and chairs. At the end of the room stood a long wooden bar. To the right was a huge dining area fit for royalty. As I entered the room, I glanced down at my watch to see what time it was. Just past noon. Glancing back up, my eyes were caught by the most gorgeous woman I had ever seen. She had on a nineteenth-century green and white dress that stood out against her ivory skin and shockingly curly red hair that fell against her bare shoulders. She was young, attractive, and as vivacious as any woman could be. My heart skipped a beat as I looked at her. She smiled a deep, long smile and looked straight at me. The dark pools in her eyes never seemed to find a bottom. She was at least a hundred feet away from me and behind the bar, and as I approached her, I was caught by her gaze.

Feeling extremely lucky to have this beautiful bar waitress all to myself, I ordered a beer and asked what was good. She smiled and let me know that she was sometimes, but for lunch, I should try the green chili stew. She and I laughed, and my masculine spirit soared. As she prepared my lunch, I thought of clever things I could say to her, hoping to make her laugh. I shouldn't have bothered. She was a genuine, sweet girl from Fort Worth, Texas and had been working at the lodge for a few years, and now, she looking to go back if she could just catch a break. I listened to her stories and fell in love with her. She smiled and laughed as she served me beer. I was in heaven.

But eventually, it began to dawn on me that a beautiful girl such as this must have to be with someone, and I had to find out as casually as I could how serious she was, or if I was being played. I posed a question, ostensibly to show her my caring and good character, about her predicament in getting back to Fort Worth and as to what was holding her back. I sat back and listened. Well, yes, she admitted she did have a boyfriend, but he was not too attentive and not around very much because of his job as a logger. Her eyes caught mine, and they let me know she was vulnerable, and her coquettish little smile was all I needed. I never mentioned another thing about it again and concentrated on winning her over.

After devouring the stew and multiple cold beers, I announced that I had some business—of what I knew not—and was going to Dallas soon. I could certainly be able to bring her along with me as a gentleman, of course, when all the while she and I knew what I was proposing to do. She looked at me with those blue doe eyes that pleaded for salvation and let me know she would think about it. I knew what that meant. I asked her what had brought her out to New Mexico in the first place, and she told me it was the wind. We both laughed, and for a moment, I dropped the subject. Yet for some reason, my stomach twisted, telling me something wasn't right. This was too perfect. She didn't seem to mind what I did or what I said. And when she looked at me with those kind eyes, I felt assured in my own virility and nobleness.

Somehow, I was in a perfect dream. I continued to drink as she served me more beers.

She let me know she was off work soon and that if I wanted a room, she could arrange it for me and bring me up there. I hastily agreed. Business could wait one more day I figured. She came back with a key and a smile. As I got up from the bar stool, I swayed a bit from all the beers and flirting and breathed deeply. She let me know that Room 18 was available, and she would show it to me. God I was hoping she would show it to me. And she did. She showed all of it to me in the most submissive, passionate style a man could ever ask for. And of course, the dream continued with the most restful sleep I had ever had. The only thing I heard all night was the slow drip of the rain on the roof. By the time morning arrived, she was gone, and although my head pounded from the alcohol, I never felt so invigorated in my life. I was a man. A conqueror reveling in his glory.

I left the hotel and went back to the gas station. I saw the Navajo woman through the window and pined to let her know of my exploits the day before and show her what a man I was. I walked between the potato chips and bean dip with my shoulders thrown back, a swagger in every step. I grabbed a fruit juice with unwavering authority and strolled up to the register. I smiled. She smiled back.

"Hey, thanks for that tip yesterday about the lodge," I said, wanting to remind her of what she had told me, and I smugly smiled.

Because she did not say anything but smiled back, I continued with my story like a peacock crowing in the wind. I let her know everything and smiled so proudly that I could barely hear her when she asked what time it was. I thought this was an extremely annoying response to my boasting, but at least I could show off my watch. I looked for the time, but my watch was gone! It was a Presidential Bulova from the turn of the century, worth quite a pretty penny, and it was missing. Had she noticed I was missing my watch? I looked up to see the Navajo woman smiling at me as I rushed out of the convenience store.

***

As I got to the lodge, I rushed in the front doors, and I didn't know what time it was.

The woman at the concierge desk smiled at me and asked how she could help. I explained to her that I had been here yesterday and that I had a room, Room 18, and that I had left my watch and was merely going upstairs to retrieve it. I smiled assuredly at her. She grinned back with a crooked smile of concern and alarm.

"Um, Sir. Room 18 has not been occupied for 100 years since the unfortunate disappearance of Rebecca. She is something of a local legend around here. Did you mean another room?"

I stopped smiling. I looked at her with consternation and a stern look of authority to let her know that I was not to be trifled with and that I had the key in my pocket. Producing it caused her to yelp in surprise, and she ran to get the hotel manager. As both of them walked out of the main office, they looked at me with a mixture of both fear and curiosity.

The manager asked me how I had gotten the key, and I told what had happened the day before. But now, instead of the story feeling like the triumph that it previously was, it somehow felt tainted, like some sort of sordid trail of tears. I finished up my story quickly. She turned to me and let me know that my story was highly improbable since the hotel had been closed for roof leak repairs yesterday and that she knew of no other key that could fit in the lock other than the one she now held in her hand. I showed her my key and assured her we should try it because I had left my expensive watch there. To my great relief, the key I had worked. As we entered Room 18, I saw my watch on the nightstand and let out a sigh of relief. That is when I glanced to the wall where the oil painting of the red-haired woman in the green and white dress from the night before smiled back at me. The hair on the back of my neck stood up. I knew even before I asked who it was in the picture. The manager let me know that she was Rebecca, the ghost that haunted the lodge. She had been caught fooling around with another man and had been killed by her extremely jealous boyfriend when he had found out. It was right at about this time I grabbed my watch and ran out of the hotel.

What a fool I had been. How could I not notice that nobody else was at the hotel? Or that there were no other customers the whole day? Or that she never minded anything I did? And who was that Navajo woman that sent me here?

In a whisper of the wind blowing through the trees and in the blink of the eye, I found myself back at the gas station, staring at the Navajo woman who peered back at me with raven's eyes.

I shouted at her, "You knew that lodge was haunted and closed, and you sent me there yesterday! Why did you do it?"

She smiled at me a long time and asked me a question, "Are you from here now?"

I stumbled out of the convenience store into the whipping wind, not sure of myself, hating that Navajo woman for what she had done to me.

Cry of the Ptarmigan

Nestled softly within its grass burrow that was bordered by a rock outcropping, the ptarmigan knew it was time to set out upon its long journey. It rubbed its neck against its mate's, in a gentle way, and set out into the sky. Flying up against the wind, she could feel the cold air flowing down from the Arctic, which lifted her high into the sky and shot her toward the ocean. Hovering over the vast and seemingly endless ocean, she could see other birds fighting for a space within the air channels that drove them up and down, the immense pressure of the wind currents battering them.

She had just laid two eggs a few months ago, and now, she had her first children. They were a boy and a girl, and she was so proud of them that she garbled and cooed incessantly into the wind to each of her neighbors. They were clumsy, full of life, and looked at her with a child's love that melted her heart. She felt fulfilled yet also very scared and responsible for their well-being— for the first few weeks, she did not leave them, not even for a second. There were always foxes and snakes and other scavengers that would be more than happy to take advantage of the defenseless young chicks. Now that she was a grown bird, she wasn't as scared of eagles as when she was young, but she knew they were looking for an easy meal as well.

Her husband was a strong bird and showed her a nice amount of affection. But now that she had born her first brood, she was angry at him for having to leave them unattended for so long to get food. Even though she knew in the back of her mind that it was not his fault, that hunting for fish took a long time, she complained at him incessantly when he came back. She could tell he was wary of seeing her once he made his way back to the nest, each time his eyes a little more distant and uncaring. She asked him why it took so long and where had he been, even though she knew he was over the ocean diving for fish. She was claustrophobic, the pressure of having to be a new mother and keep guard over her children pressing in on her. She loved them with all her heart and yet desired to be free as well. She was experiencing the joys and pains of being a new mother.

Rising into the wind, she felt free and alive again. She had let her husband look after the chicks for the first time, and she relished in the joy of being one with nature. She rose and dipped downward with the air currents, even twirled a time or two in the air just because it felt so good. She was a free bird to do as she wished. Seeing a fish down below in the water, she knew the meal was hers for the taking. Plummeting toward the water, she drove straight into the sea and nabbed the unknowing fish before it realized what had happened. Bringing it back to the shore, she ate heartily and with such a force of instinct and reckless abandon that she almost coughed from her large gulping bites. Now that she had eaten and felt satiated from the meal, she took some time for herself to enjoy the last rays of the morning sun. The sun felt good on her back, and she contemplated going back, but she felt so content that she decided to relax for just a few more moments until she could catch her breath.

She did not want to go back to the nest just yet, even though she felt compelled to return. It was a curious feeling to have freedom mixed with maternal love and responsibility. The two feelings tugged at one another, and she thought of her mate. He was a very strong and responsible mate who looked out for her and now looked after their children. She trusted him—he had never done her wrong. They had met while on Atka Island a little more than three months ago. He had beautiful plumage and had shown her his dance steps and flight moves that made her breast flutter. There was something special about him that attracted her to him, and she could not resist his entreaties.

Their mating happened numerous times, and she knew she was with child within a week. She had never felt this way before, so fulfilled and content with life.

And then it came time to carry the eggs and the discomfort that came with it. She had complained a bit, but knew this was the way of all female ptarmigans and so held the burden against her heart like all new pregnant mothers did. Eventually, it came time to lay her eggs. Her mate had made her a special place on an outcropping close to the others but far enough away that she could have some privacy. The outcropping was on a ledge that rose three hundred feet up from the crashing sea. It was indented into the cliff and just big enough for a family to be comfortable and yet not so big as to allow any other animal to claim it as their own.

The grass and straw and bits of needles he had brought to make the nest had made it soft and yet firm. He had done a splendid job, and how proud they both were. They were in love, and all of their problems rose into the wind and disappeared like the smoke from a distant volcano. They had each other and soon would be a family. When it was time, she laid her two eggs and sat on them religiously while he went and hunted for their breakfast, lunch, and dinner. He was a good provider, and she was pleased with her choice. Even though she felt constricted by having to stay on the nest, she also felt wonderful inside knowing that soon she would see the fruit of her body when the eggs hatched. She was just as pleased with her husband who fed her and continued to fight off any predators that came near their nest.

And then her chicks hatched. A joy she had never known enveloped her mind and body. She was no longer one but three! Her life was now split into multiple little chicks that looked into her eyes and asked for everything without knowing anything. But they knew she was their mother. They squawked and chittered and cooed like all birds do and told her of their wants and needs and, eventually, of their love. She was as much a part of them as her wings were to her. Desperately, she wanted everything that was the best for them, and her love knew no boundaries. She was experiencing a mother's love.

But somehow, her relationship with her mate had changed. When he came back from hunting and gathering for the family, it was different. She felt less in love with him and began to wonder if it had been more lustful because of her desires prior to giving birth to the children. The demands of their children and the care that it took to keep them happy was more stressful than she ever imagined. She felt trapped in an invisible cage. They had never had this problem prior to the children, but eventually, it became evident to him that he had been usurped by his own children. He accepted this demotion with the love that a father has for his children and just hoped and prayed that she could see one day how life really was.

This had gone on for days, and then weeks, without anything getting better. In fact, it got much worse. Yes, the children were thriving and getting stronger and were happy, but they were squabbling. She knew he had tried to make things better by bringing back the most exquisite morsels of fish he could find, but even this had not helped. Once, he had even fought off an eagle, with his shrieks and dives, driving it away from the ledge they lived on, but still, she became unhappy once again a few days after the incident. She needed freedom. Finally, after a month, he was allowed to care for the chicks, who were now almost half his size, and told her to have fun and be careful. He could feel her frustration blooming from her confinement, but she could not seem to understand or feel the enormous pressure he was under to care for the family, all the while protecting himself and them.

On the beach, enjoying her first self-caught meal in over a month, it felt luxurious to have a family and two wonderful children, and she began to think about her husband, who she had been giving so much grief lately. As she thought about it, it dawned on her that this was really what life was all about and that her parents must have gone through much of the same experiences. She felt a little bad for how she had treated him recently and vowed to be better to him. He really was trying hard. Absentmindedly, she began to think of what she could bring back for dinner. She was feeling very good and relaxed and flapped up off of the shore, beginning to head her beak into the wind, above the breakers that were crashing down upon the shoreline. She kept her eyes intently upon the water, looking for a tasty fish, like a mackerel or a cod or perhaps a small tuna. As she focused her eyes on the water below, she finally saw something that attracted her attention. Flying like she had in her youth, before she had given birth, she swooped down. Skimming just below the surface of the water was a supreme delicacy of a fish, if only she could get there in time.

As she began to make her final descent, she noticed something out of the corner of her eye. An eagle's talon! Before she could react, it ripped into her side, and she felt herself being lifted high into the air in its grasp. Although she struggled with all of her might, she had no hope. The eagle was ten times her size. The intensity and joy of freedom she had been experiencing had distracted her, made her forget about the peripheral vision that usually kept her safe from predators. Carried off into the wind to the eagle's nest, she became the tasty meal that she had hoped to catch. Her kids would never see her again. And neither would her husband, who had warned her to be careful before she had left.

As it approached sundown, anxiously, hoping that nothing had happened to her, he kept scanning the sky for the look of her familiar body. By eight in the evening, he believed he knew what had happened. He kept crying out into the wind, hoping that she would appear, but her voice was only in his memory now. And he could not do anything about it. He surmised that he had lost her to an eagle, and he knew he may lose the kids as well because he could not hunt while guarding them. He was distraught beyond any pain he had ever felt before in his life. And to make matters worse, the children were complaining to him that their mother was missing and that they were hungry. He regurgitated what he could for them into their empty bellies, albeit a very small amount of fish gruel, but at least it got them to sleep.

During the night, his mind wandered in confusion. He was alone with two children who could not be left alone without protection from predators, but yet he had to hunt to feed them. It seemed an impossible job. He felt so alone with the weight of the mountains upon his shoulders. Looking up into the night sky, he looked for some solace in the familiar stars that had guided him upon many journeys, but tonight, they did not seem to shine as bright, and his heart was filled with pain. He knew she was gone forever. He imagined her looking down upon him at that moment from heaven, far up in the sky beyond a mortal bird's reach. He looked down at the two peacefully resting chicks who unbeknownst to them had been given a death sentence as well that day. He felt sad and lost as the night air cut between his feathers and chilled his body. He convinced himself to sleep and, at least for one more night, to keep their children safe and warm.

During his sleep, he dreamed that she was with him. She spoke gently to him, like when they were courting each other, but they did not touch each other. She was there in front of him, and he knew it was her spirit speaking to him. She let him know she was sorry for the way she had acted of late and that she forgave him as well. He felt comforted by her words but lost, unable to say anything back. She smiled and let him know she had to leave and that he should take care of the children as best he could. The answers to his questions could be found in their children's eyes, if he looked hard enough. She turned and flew away. A panic struck him, and he struggled to catch her and make her explain herself before she left, but she was already gone, flying high up into the stars.

The pale gray of the dawn began creeping across the eastern horizon. He found himself staring off into space. He knew he must get some food for him and his children. But how? The girl chick, Atta, awoke first and nestled next to him as he stood on the ledge, looking out at the water with its whitecaps rhythmically pushing toward the shore. He felt her warmth, and the ice that had recently grown on his heart melted. He was hurt and angry, and he felt her love. He looked down and saw the sadness in her eyes as well, and he knew that she understood what had happened to her mother. And yet even as a child, she was giving him strength through her own pain. For the first time in over a day, he breathed deeply and vowed to try and find a way to protect her and her brother. With a smile born of love, he looked into her eyes and saw the fear she was feeling. He knew now he must be strong for all of them if they were to survive. He led her back to her brother and put her back in the nest. Cooing softly, he let her know he would be back soon.

He flew out into the sky across the depths of the ocean and easily pulled in a fish within a few minutes. Quickly, he returned to the nest, and already found his son teetering off the side of the ledge. He pecked him into submission like he had never done before. His daughter watched curiously, learning the lesson. He got them their breakfast and let them know to be diligent and stay on the ledge no matter what happened. They were happy with their first real meal in over a day. He was just happy that one essential chore of the day had been accomplished. This would keep them on the nest for a while. He now thought he understood what his wife's spirit had talked to him about. There was no time to lose.

He flew off again, and instead of searching the ocean for food, he chose to make his way to the thousands of ptarmigans nesting on the beach. He landed and began to walk around the nests that crowded the seashore and were filled with the cries of baby chicks. He walked and walked. He saw many of them looking at him curiously, some with a fair amount of hostility. He continued to walk. And then, after more than an hour, he saw a female ptarmigan who appeared to be lost. She was looking up and down the shoreline with a look of desperation and blind hope. He watched her but did not approach. After some time, she noticed him.

He asked her if he could help in any way, and she cooed back that she had lost her only chick and could not find her. He asked if she had been to her nest and looked, and she replied that she had, over twenty times, and that still her chick was missing. She was afraid that it had been snatched by an eagle or fox or some other hungry animal and let him know that her husband had been killed just recently, forcing her to leave the nest to hunt for food for her newborn. He looked at her and let her know his wife had been taken by an eagle on her last hunting trip, and he was now all alone with newborn chicks. They looked at one another, and she understood what he was saying and asking. They combed the beach for hours, looking for her child with no luck. In the end, they flew off together and joined his children. In the great search for love and life, they had chosen to survive with each other as new mates in the tough Arctic environment where they lived.

As they lay there beside the children, he knew the pain she was suffering and was grateful for her coming to stay with him. He was not enthralled with having to choose a new mate so haphazardly, but he assumed correctly that she probably wasn't really enthralled with the idea either. Rather, they were both being realistic about each of their current situations. Love might follow with time and understanding, but necessity was the meaning of today. They slept soundly upon the rock ledge. But more importantly, so did the children.

The Banjo Man

If you ever get the chance to travel to the Pocono Mountains in the heart of Pennsylvania, you might just get to hear the story of the Banjo Man. In many a log cabin bar, where eyes peer back at you from gaunt faces and limbs worn down from years of cutting timber or hard-scrabble years in the coal mines, they know of him. I would suggest you buy them a beer or two before you start asking about the Banjo Man. You see, he is a bit of a local legend, and it takes a bit of convincing to get the story out, if you catch my drift.

A long time ago, back before the Great Depression, a young man came all alone to live in the green valleys and pine tree studded mountains that encompass the hills. He was friendly enough, but mostly, he kept to himself. People said he didn't have the desire for a woman—just being alone with the wilderness was fine with him. He built himself a fine sturdy log cabin that allowed him to live happily with the forest critters and his thoughts. Some people called him hermit, and he was different, I grant you that, but it wasn't that he was un-friendly to others, just that he liked to keep his distance. And so, it went. He worked the land around him and re-ceived the grace of food from his garden and surrounding forest, and sometimes, to make ends meet, he would cut some trees and sell the chopped wood at a roadside stand. He had himself a cat named Gato, and he thrived.

The smell of the cool moss in the heat of the summer, the blooming flowers in the spring as they poked through the thinning ice, the towering trees, and the changing seasons were all like a magic potion to him that kept him alive and vibrant. And he made sure to keep it that way. You see, he had found himself a small paradise nestled next to a creek in the back mountains, far away from any roads or traffic or people. He didn't want to be disturbed by the horns or shouts or bad manners that accompanied much of human society, and he deemed himself one very lucky man. He was living with nature as part of nature and making sure he wasn't polluting any part of it. He cut trees down from different sections of the land to en-sure the vitality of everything that surrounded him, and he only fished what he could eat. He had a great rever-ence for all living creatures and had promised himself never to shoot another living creature that could stare back at him on all fours.

He was a man with nature like nothing ever seen be-fore. At night, sitting on his porch in the chill of the after-twilight air, he taught himself how to play the banjo he had gotten from his late pappy, and after a few years, he had taught himself mighty fine. He also taught himself to play the jug and the harmonica as well, but he loved the banjo the best. Sometimes, a distant neighbor would track by his cabin when he was playing, and if the neighbor knew enough to bring a few beers, then friendly conversation would likely ensue. People liked the Banjo Man and knew his heart was righteous and good. He spoke about the animals and was able to communicate with them by voice, banjo, harmonica, and jug.

In fact, he could play so well that the neighbors began to realize that the wild animals from around the area were drawn to his music. In the early evenings, before the sun dipped below the horizon, the forest surrounding his cabin was full of animals of all types. Masked-faced raccoons were foraging, deer grazing, brown chipmunks and gray and red squirrels hiding their nuts, but all with an ear to what he was playing. Meanwhile, all the different species of birds were chirping between the songs and sometimes along with the very tunes he banged out on that banjo. Around that cabin, they all seemed to move a little slower at that time of day and listen to the beautiful sounds emanating from the porch. He was a part of their forest, not separated in any way like most men's castles are set out to be. While he played on the porch, many an astonished onlooker, if they had come for a visit, would look on in amazement when a wild animal would wander inside of his cabin. The forest had adopted the Banjo Man.

If he beat out a drumming sound on the jug, he knew he could get a bear to eventually itch its back on the trees. If he lit into the banjo and twanged it real high, he could get the blue jay to screech out a reply. And if he livened up the land with a toe-tapping harmonica tune, he could get the young deer to jump off the ground and run to and fro. His senses were aligned with the rhythms and feelings of the forest and its inhabitants.

And so, it was that many years passed without anything really changing, that is, except for the seasons, the additions of the newborns, and the passing of the elders.

And then one day, it all changed. A city slicker from the Big Apple decided he needed a place to get away from his fast-paced, callous world. Buying up property on the other side of the stream from the Banjo Man, he proceeded to bring in his noise, his aggravations, his polluting truck, and, worst of all, his guns. The first thing he did was shoot one of the larger bucks that hung around the Banjo Man's property, promptly skinned it, and mounted the head and antlers on the front of his cabin. To the Banjo Man, this was a grisly sight to have to look at.

The conversation did not go well. The Banjo Man tried to make the man understand that he communed with nature and that nature was his friend, but the man would have none of it. He trampled over his protests and told him in his most powerful city voice to basically go jump in a lake. The city man had a good time telling his coworkers the following Monday what a country bump-kin he had met and how he had told him to go shove his fairy tale fantasies of living as one with nature.

The animals were afraid to come around anymore. The Banjo Man didn't blame them. For three straight weekends, the man had come up to the property on the weekends and revved his truck, set off the alarms, shot and killed whatever he could, drank beer, and blared his music from the radio. Soon, it would be spring, and the mothers with their newborns were going to be making their rounds. Worst of all, this man seemed to enjoy act-ing like an ass because he could sense it upset his neigh-bor. The Banjo Man had even overheard him while he was talking on the phone about shooting a bear. The Banjo Man was depressed.

The following weekend, the man was back again, right as spring had arrived. On Saturday morning, the man dressed in hunting greens, a large caliber rifle strapped to his back, and began his hunt for a bear. He didn't have to look far to find what he was looking for. Fresh bear scat was just upriver from his cabin. Follow-ing along for a mile, he came to what appeared to be a den. This was too easy. Soon, he would have a bearskin rug and a story to tell the people back at his office. He sat and waited for the mother and her cubs to come out. For more than three hours, he waited as the sun rose higher in the sky. It was getting hot, and he was getting restless. He put his gun to the side of the log and began to undress, taking off his hunting jacket. It was then he heard the most awful screeching sound, as though a baby bear was being butchered. Startled and surprised by the horrible screeching sound that emanated from the bear's den, he was too late in hearing the commotion behind him. He turned just in time to see a large black female bear with two cubs charging him. Desperately, he tried to pick up his gun and get off a shot, but it was too late. The bear crashed into him and ripped him apart within seconds. Spun down to the ground with blood spurting from his neck, he knew he was dead. In his last moments, he saw his bumpkin neighbor with a banjo in his hands, smiling in his direction atop the rocks of the den. And he knew he had been fooled.

As he walked back to his cabin, the Banjo Man mused that sometimes, the worst sounding music had its benefits too.

At least, that was the story that was told to me by a few of the locals at Big Bear Lodge in the Pocono Mountains.

The Potter's Field

Oh, what a dastardly cruel fate his master had bestowed upon him. He sat alone in his one-room house, carefully twining three separate pieces of rope together to make them strong enough so as not to break when the time came. And on the table, under the light of the candle that had been burning throughout the night, keeping his small home barely livable from the cold drafts of the nearby sea, lay thirty pieces of silver. The candle flickered, casting its shadows on the silvery serpents that mocked him. His family knew him as a betrayer that had turned asunder his beliefs to receive these ill-gotten gains. Only he knew differently. He had been asked by his master to tell the truth and to set his master free. But, oh, what pain he felt for having obeyed him!

It had been a long night, and his hands were stiff and sore from making the rope, and yet, he continued with the laborious work because he knew that soon it would be sunrise. And then, he would be free. It was cold in the house, and he shivered from the lack of warmth in his body and spirit. At first, he could not understand why his master had asked him to do such a horrible thing, but a day's reflecting had brought a sharp realization. He had known all along that the end would come, and his master had merely set the time of his own demise. Yes, he could have run, but that was not his way, and he knew this in his heart. Instead, as the circle had tightened around them, his master had asked of him a favor, and he had given it, although not without trying to understand why, beseeching his master to take this burden away from him.

By giving himself up, his master had given his brother and friends freedom. This he knew to be true in his heart. But what else was there, now that he was gone, except for his teachings and the thoughts they held of him? The misery was black upon his mind, and his heart felt heavy like a stone. He heard the first signs of the morning as a rooster crowed somewhere in the surrounding darkness. He had all night to think about what he was going to do with his newfound wealth, and the solution had been difficult, but one must live with one's actions. Yes, that was good—he had learned something from his master after all.

His mind was but a blur of different thoughts and images from the past few days. The evil he had seen on people's faces had contrasted with the weeping of those in pain. This damn world was an abomination, and he would show them. Or maybe they would not care one iota and continue on with their wicked ways. But as he finished up the length of rope that was spread out before him on the modest wooden table, he knew that it was time to make things right.

Grabbing up the silver, he dropped it in a small pouch slung off his belt. They were ice cold to his touch, and yet strangely, they felt like hot coals upon his hands. He hated these pieces of metal, each stamped with the authority of power that pulled like a yoke around everyone's neck. He shivered from the thoughts that ran through his head. It was time. It was good that it was time. Pushing back the rug that hung in his doorway, he carried with him the rope and the silver and started the long trek toward town. Nobody was up at this hour but the roosters and himself, and he gazed at the stars and wondered what it was like to be free. Free from hate, free from pain, free from greed, free from tyranny, free from desire. What was it truly like to be free? He relished the thought of giving oneself up to complete submission. The thought swept over his mind like a huge wave washing over him, cleansing his mind.

In this state, he did not notice the cold of the night air or the jackal that eyed him suspiciously, nor the boy asleep, supposedly herding sheep in the pasture. By the time dawn was breaking, he had reached the village square. He could see that many of the stalls were already doing business and that others were getting ready to start up for the day. Food for money, animals for money, wares for money, slaves for money, even money for money. The merchants were licking their chops—the den of thieves was open for business. He could see that some of them had stopped to stare at him, and some within the walls pointed. Some had smirks upon their faces while others cast him false smiles, seeing the money purse busting with the treasure they so dearly wanted. Passing among them, he finally reached the money traders. Stopping and standing before them, he hurled the silver among them as they stood and stared at him in disbelief.

"Here is your death. Here is your God. Grab it for all of your sins and for all of your fathers' and sons' sins as well."

Later that day, they found him swinging from a rope. To this day, there is a story among those who cut him down and buried him. You see, in his face lay the smile of a man who had reached a higher spiritual place.

The Three Cards

On the second of September, the white card came innocuously enough: through the mail, like any other letter. It didn't say anything. From the front to the middle pages to the back, it was completely blank. Furthermore, there was no return address, only being addressed to Ms. Courtney McFee. When she had gotten her mail that day, she had thought nothing of it. It was curious, nonetheless, that she should receive something without any marking or rhyme or reason, but mistakes do happen. She had studied the postmark and couldn't imagine who would be sending her something from New York City. The postmark was addressed from Manhattan, and the card was an expensive card stock of ivory white linen that was presumably of the twenty pound paper stock. Curious, but life goes on, so she dismissed it, throwing it into the trash. She had a husband to dominate, an ex to destroy, and a family to manipulate until she received most, if not all, of the family's inheritance. She was a walking psychopath with the utmost confidence in her ability to destroy people and their relationships and get whatever she desired. And she desired money, and the power that came with it, above all. Furthermore, she wanted the destruction of everyone she thought had harmed her. And to this point in her life, she was getting her way by all means necessary. She was a master liar, manipulator, thief, con artist, philanderer, and fraud. She had conned men, government organizations, housing authorities, her parents, supposed friends, and lovers out of everything she could and then looked upon them with disgust.

A few weeks after receiving the letter, while on the phone with her mother and incessantly talking about herself and the fools around her, she stopped and heard something her mother said.

"Wait, did you say you received a blank card in the mail?"

"Yes dear, I don't know what to make of it. It was on very fine paper and had no markings on it whatsoever!" Her mother said this with nervous apprehension.

"I got one too! Oh my God . . . Do you remember where it came from? Was it addressed by anyone?"

"Well, dear, that is a curious thing. It had no return address, but it came from New York City. And quite frankly, I can't remember knowing anyone from there? Isn't that the strangest thing? I am a bit concerned about the whole thing."

A blank card by itself was no big deal, or was it? Maybe it was a mistake by a printing company that had both of them on their mailing list? Surely, it meant nothing, but still, they pondered who they knew in the city or what scoundrel was trying to get one over on them.

The conversation went on for another twenty minutes, but Courtney was not involved. Her mind was racing back and forth trying to figure out who was playing games with her and her family. By the end of the day, she thought she had figured it out. Her brother and sister had already received blank white cards by mail, and the only one who would probably go to such lengths was her ex-husband. She had screwed him over for child support for nearly twenty years, had taken him to court on false charges more times than she could count, and had destroyed his relationship with their only son. It must be him.

But then again, it might be her old best friend, the person she had betrayed by snatching her boyfriend away. It was not that she wanted him for any long-term relationship—she just hated being second fiddle to a couple in the throngs of love. She hated love, and people who were in love, because she felt none of it. Perhaps, though, it was her ex-coworker, the man she had made subtle advances on in the break room. She had teased him and cajoled him and finally had him so wound up that he couldn't stop himself from making a move on her. She had him fired for sexual misconduct within a few weeks and had secured his job within a month. It served him right, the dumb lecherous idiot.

Over the coming days, the card bothered her to extreme lengths. She made inquiries, none of them direct of course, but she checked up with employers and social media sites and found that none of them were anywhere near where the envelopes had been mailed. It was becoming more and more disturbing. Who was it? She began to make a list of everyone she had ever wronged and felt could hold a grudge. By the time she had listed twenty people, she decided that she had had enough. But she couldn't stop. She was soon checking every person on the list, looking into their whereabouts on the day the cards were postmarked. Nobody was going to get the upper hand on her. Ever! The research continued for weeks until, fruitlessly, it came to an end. She decided that she was just being neurotic and that it had all been some printer's mistake.

It was exactly two months later that the black card arrived in the mail. It was postmarked from Mequon, Wisconsin. The front, the middle pages, and the back were all completely blank. It was a fine heavy paper with deckle edges and postmarked on the second of November. The panic that arose within her had her calling everyone she had ever wronged and threatening them. Whether it was done by phone, by voicemail, or text, she reached out to everyone that she had ever screwed over and accused them of assaulting her sensibilities. She threatened and yelled at each of them, but to no avail. No one was interested in hearing from her, much less being accused of such a ridiculous stunt as mailing her and her family blank cards from different parts of the country. On many a phone call, she was hung up on.

Her parents and siblings were at a loss as to who the mystery mailer could be, but they seemed much less concerned with it than her. They just didn't understand that this was an affront to her personal well-being, that they were merely pawns in the game being played on her. Or maybe they did understand, and it was of no concern to them? She thought of mailing all of her enemy's blank cards and then realized how foolish that would look because she had already contacted most of them. Damn it. Someone was getting the best of her, knew it, and was probably laughing at her expense. If only she knew who her enemy was, she could best him or her, but this game just wasn't fair.

Within days, the postal service had been contacted. She had been rebuffed in trying to get them involved because she was under no threat, at least not from a blank card. She even paid the money to have the card analyzed for fingerprints by a private detective, but the card must have been handled with gloves because there were no fingerprints to be found. It was frustrating to the point where she couldn't concentrate. She was losing sleep, not being productive at work, and had felt the fire of hatred that usually burned bright within her soul take a turn toward fear, wariness, and extreme bitterness. She knew this couldn't continue—it was consuming her whole being.

New Years was not a joyous celebration for her. She knew she would get a card the next day, and it was making her insane. All night long, she stayed awake, restlessly trying not to think of what was coming in the mail. She took off work the next day, waiting for the mailman. When he came, she met him at her mailbox. With an almost simmering anger, she asked if he had anything for her. Taken aback a bit, he handed over her mail. She snatched it without a thank you and turned back toward her house. By the time she was inside, she was trembling. It was a stack of magazines and leaflets and bills and nothing more! She looked it over again as fast as her hands could move. There was no envelope, no blank card. Nothing was there. The greatest sense of relief and triumph swept over her body. She wanted so badly to believe that the cruel joke was over. For an instant, she almost felt joy in her heart, but then remembered how miserable the past few months had been. That was when the bitter feeling of revenge washed over her. That was what she wanted, her ultimate friend, revenge. The mix of emotions had her so unraveled that she didn't know what to do. She wanted to call someone to tell them, but who could she call besides her family, many of whom had stopped picking up her calls?

A month later, on February second, she received a blank red card. It had no postmark on the envelope, and none of the members of her family had received one. She had known all along her family had been included just to fool her. Evil knows evil. The stalker must have hand-delivered the card to her mailbox. He or she was there in town waiting for her. With her blinds drawn, peeping out from the shadows, she saw everyone and hated them all. Previously, she had perceived everyone as her pawn, fool, and easy mark. Now, she was their fool, their pawn. She was angry and beside herself and scared of whom-ever had been stalking her. Three simple blank cards had changed everything.

The Prospector

For thirty years, he had prospected the land. He had caught the fever when he had been a young kid and never could shake the urge to hunt for that elusive gold. He had found some golden nuggets early on by dumb luck, and it had ensnared him like a perpetual gambler at the horse races. It had been his land ever since he had bought it in 1905 for twenty-five dollars, the remains of an inheritance after his pappy had passed away. But the years had been tough on him, the winters and the work beginning to make his bones feel like the gnarled poplar trees that stood guard above the stream that ran through his property. It was over one hundred acres of beautiful pine trees, the rock and bear country in the northern highlands of New Mexico. Five years after he had bought the land, the territory had become a state. He had never had a wife and would not be able to get one if he tried. He had always told himself that as soon as he hit it big, he would find someone. He would come down from the mountains with a wheelbarrow full of gold and then get the most beautiful woman in the land and live on a ranch with his riches. But it didn't work out that way. He had worked tirelessly, panning and digging, barely scratching out a living that any sensible woman would faint at the thought of. The years had played tricks on him. Time had flown by with his pick and shovel—his two best friends—and that damn elusive hope of striking it big always was there in the back of his mind. How he wished he had never found those pieces of gold when he was younger. Oh, how he wished.

In his cabin, he had one mirror, its luster faded by the passing of time, and as he looked at himself, he saw a wrinkled old man with a frayed cowboy hat blankly staring out at him. He thought he saw his father—the look the man had right before passing away—looking back at him. He sat down on his sparse wooden bed that he had made hundreds of moons ago, back when he was spry and his hands worked well and his bones didn't ache from the cold. He didn't want to give up the fight and have to admit that he had been wrong all his life about there being gold in the hills, but his body was not up to the task anymore. Not to mention, he knew he had to go see a doctor about a pain that wouldn't go away in his belly, and he needed money to do that. The problem was that he didn't own anything but the land he had bought over fifty years ago.

The land was like the wife and kids he never had. It hurt him to even think of parting with it, but then the hurt came back to his belly, and the reality of the threadbare cabin made the pain even greater. He would be forced to sell some of his land just to live.

And so, it was.

The townspeople were surprised when they happened to glimpse the old hermit prospector on his unlikely visits into the town. Many had called him a fool all of these years, and the years had proven them right. Reluctantly, he tramped up to the local real estate office and made a contract to sell one-quarter of his holdings, about twenty-five acres. He was asking one thousand dollars an acre. The agent tried explaining to him that comparable properties were going for half as much, but he wouldn't listen to it. There was a reason the people in town called him a curmudgeonly old fool. Needless to say, the fall turned to winter and winter to spring, and still, he had no offers on his property. With every passing day, the pain in his belly kept getting worse, making him wince at times, and the bitterness inside of him frothed like the bile he spat up. He was a wrecked and wretched old man.

In the spring, with just the whistling of the birds to accompany him in his loneliness, he peeked out the window and happened to see a man approaching his cabin. It was the real estate agent! By God, he might just have a sale! He got up off his bed so fast he felt the pain hit him, but all the same, he was at the door within seconds, using the help of a long, wooden homemade cane. After greetings were exchanged, the agent pulled out a surveyor's map of the property and showed him what acreage his client was willing to purchase. It was incredible. He had finally found a bigger sucker than he was. The piece the man wanted to buy was bordered by a humongous rock that diverted the stream back onto the remaining seventy-five acres he would still own. That land had, at most, a mile's worth of stream upon it, and it never had given him anything more than a backache and a few grains of gold. This was by far the most useless piece of the property he owned, and someone was willing to pay full price! He wanted to tell the real estate agent what he knew, but he didn't want to sabotage the deal, so he stayed quiet and felt a warm feeling in his belly. Some of his bitterness subsided, knowing he was finally getting the better of someone else.

On the day of the closing, he decided to stick around the town so he could see who had bought his worthless piece of land at such a high price. Besides, he had an appointment with the doctor. After seeing the doctor, he was relieved but angry. He was going to live, but he needed surgery. The surgery would cost exactly what he had just received from the sale of his property. He surmised that the real estate agent must have spoken to the doctor about the sale of his property because the price of the surgery matched exactly what he was going to receive from the sale of this land. He felt like he had been screwed again. They were in cahoots together. But alas, there was nothing he could do about it. So, he stuck around town at a local diner situated just across from the real estate agent, giving him a direct view of who was coming and going. For once, he would treat himself to meal.

An hour later, a young man in his twenties walked up the front steps of the agent's office and signed some papers. The deal was done. Then, much to his chagrin and good fortune, the man walked over to the diner and sat along the counter and ordered lunch. He was full of himself and his books and papers. He talked to the waitress about how he had just bought some prime land up in the mountains and was going to go prospecting for gold. He had done all his research and studied the land and had bought all the tools he needed to strike it rich. He even said that if he struck it rich, he would be back into town and buy himself a ranch and retire.

Quiet as a church mouse and sucking it all in like he was eating a delicious dessert, the prospector listened intently to the story of his youth being retold by a younger version of himself. Deep inside, the old prospector couldn't help but laugh at the foolish young boy. How he longed to tell him what a rube he was for buying that "prime" piece of property, which he knew was worthless. How much he wanted to tell him how little there was on the land to sustain a man, but he was getting a sick sort of pleasure from watching someone else suffer from the ignorance and greed that comes from catching gold fever. So, he sat and listened and cherished every moment of the delusional words flowing from the young man's mouth.

The pain in his belly was gone, but the bitterness still remained. They had stolen a part of him and his profits, from the land he had owned almost his entire life. The simple operation had lasted two hours. It was highway robbery, and he knew it, but there was nothing he could do about it but grumble to himself as he made his way back to his cabin. He had spent a week in town recuperating and now found himself without any joy except thinking of the young man and how he must be struggling with his new endeavor. He decided that the next day, he would go over to that part of his property and meet his new neighbor.

The following morning, he was up early and rode his only horse north to the huge stone that separated the properties. The stone must have weighed over five tons and was an unusual feature among the landscape. Over the centuries, many had carved their initials or drawn upon the rock, letting others know that they had visited this patch of wilderness. As he nudged his horse along the well-beaten trails toward the rock, he began to notice that some activity had already taken place. A few trees were cut down, and the branches had been cut off of them. They were now thirty foot long logs. Straight ahead of him was the young man, sawing the trees in half. He wondered what he was doing although he realized the young man was probably building a cabin like the old prospector had done years before. A grin spread across his face.

The young man stopped when he saw him approaching and waved. Getting down from his horse, the old prospector smiled and shook the man's hand.

"Aren't you the guy that sold me the property?"

"I sure am. The name is Ben, short for Benjamin Dodge."

"Well, I sure am glad you sold this property to me. I am going to make my fortune off of it, and then, I am going to buy me a large ranch and get me a little lady and have me a family. This place is beautiful, and according to my maps and charts, there is gold in these hills! I have been studying how to look for the right signs and clues as to where the gold is, and I believe this is the right spot."

Before he could say anymore, Ben burst out laughing so much so that it began to hurt his belly. The young man just stared and looked at him with a curious wonderment. In his glee at meeting a fool greater than himself, he forgot all about being civil. All the vitriol and scorn he had endured for years came lashing out of his body.

"You damned young fool. This here property has been scoured for gold, and there ain't nothing here! I know 'cause I have looked over here for over fifty years, and you bought the most worthless piece of scrub land that ever could be bought and paid twice the going rate. I must admit, though, that you remind me of myself when I was your age. Just twice as dumb."

After the outburst, there wasn't much more conversation to be had. Ben returned home to his cabin and gloated over the way the young man's face fell flat when he told him the truth. It was almost a month later when Ben happened to be up in that region and heard shouts like a war party fixing to charge. Angling his horse up into the mountains, he noticed something was wrong but couldn't quite put his finger on it. He was looking for the rock, and it wasn't there! Had somebody moved the rock? Silently, he plodded his horse up to the northeast so that he could get a better look at the scene from above where the rock used to sit.

Looking down, he could see that the rock had been toppled onto its side and there was a hole where it used to sit. The young man, the real estate agent, and the doctor were all crowded around something. That was when one of them stood up, and the glint of the gold nearly blinded him off of his saddle. They were picking up handfuls of golden coins and dropping them back into the chest that lay on the ground between them. And then he heard their voices.

"Santa Ana's lost treasure . . . just like the maps said it would be. Right next to the large rock that diverts the stream with the initials SA carved upon it. We are rich! We are all filthy rich!"

Ben didn't remember the ride home or that he tidied up his place prior to pulling out his revolver.

The shot that rang out in the cabin, only disturbed the birds momentarily from their warbling songs.

The Spy?

He was a spy. And he was growing old and tired of the constant cat and mouse game. He had been running the domestic terrorism unit for the past twelve years, which consisted of spying on citizens from his own country, ones deemed to be enemies of the state. Sometimes, the job ended in an assassination. But mostly, it was laborious, time-consuming work that involved thousands of hours of surveillance and sometimes—only sometimes—did he actually catch the perpetrator. Often, the foreign agent left his district of authority, and the case had to be transferred to another unit commander in another part of the country or even to an overseas unit. The work was tedious, a thankless job considering he was an undercover agent of the state. He took photographs, made copious notes, talked into his lapel, where a hidden recorder lay, and created thousands of files on suspected terrorists. He made cases against individuals that could hold up in a court of law. In his years of service, he had uncovered numerous domestic and international plots against individuals, governments, and leaders of organizations. Often, it involved the smuggling of goods, human trafficking, narcotics, and other nefarious underworld activities run by clandestine organizations that laundered vast amounts of money through sophisticated networks. The money that was being channeled through these networks sometimes dwarfed the annual GDP of small nations, while on other occasions, it was the leading politicians of the government that were secretly siphoning off the taxpayers' money in illegal schemes. It was a frustrating job fraught with danger that had him constantly on edge, always looking over his shoulder to see if anyone had him in their sights.

He had entered the army when he was young, just out of high school, and had fought in the Iraqi wars, witnessing an inordinate amount of death and destruction. The screams of people in shock, from losing a limb to an improvised explosive device, or having been riddled with bullets by a sniper, were permanently etched into his mind, like a recording that could play whenever silence came to accompany him. Eventually, he had transitioned into a counter-intelligence unit and had become schooled in the arts of surveillance, deception, and killing. On many an occasion, the choice was simple: either death to others or to him, and, of course, he was still the one walking around to tell his story. But that didn't mean that he had survived unscathed. He walked with a bit of a limp from a deep knife wound taken in his left thigh years ago in Belarus. He had also lost the tip of his pinkie finger in an alley fight in Singapore when a metal door was slammed shut on his hand, slicing it clean off. But for the most part, he had been the lucky one, or more skilled, depending on the point of view.

He realized that his best years were behind him. In his mind, you needed three things in the profession to survive: skill, a sound mind and body, and a bit of luck. The skill came from years of watching others' failings and having an innate sense of knowing when to be cautious and when to be reckless. The luck was just that, but the more missions he took, the more he knew that one day the dice would roll snake eyes. Finally, the art of fighting one's opponent oftentimes came down to a quicker eye, a stronger move, or quicker jab, and the competition was getting better. The onset of age was running against him. He knew he couldn't beat the clock. No one ever did.

The other problem was the pay. He had been working for so long off-the-grid that his contacts in Washington were almost all gone. Even in the best of times, the pay had been sporadic, only based upon completed missions, but as of late, he hadn't seen anything show up in his post office box for years. True, he knew he was a mercenary in many respects and lived much like an animal in the wild, but his repeated requests to get paid had gone unanswered. If he didn't hear from his superiors soon, he would have to travel to the east coast and get some answers from the higher ups in Langley or DC. He had back pay coming to him, and looking at his graying hairs in his shaving mirror, he realized it was almost time to retire. Luckily, some of the stiffs that he had knocked off recently had quite a bit of cash on them. Keeping the money he found was one of the perks of the job.

While cooking some breakfast on his camp stove, high up in the desert wilderness that surrounded the region he patrolled, he decided that he would call Colonel Whatley one more time and try to get some answers. He had left the colonel multiple messages in the past year without any answer. He was getting irritated about the whole state of affairs and wanted some answers. He didn't carry a cell phone, obviously, so he knew he would have to use one of the old pay telephones that still existed in certain parts of the city. Stuffing items into his backpack, he began the long hike out of the mountains, making his way toward the city lights that shined orange in the predawn hours of the day. By noon, sweating and dehydrated, he had reached a payphone inside of an old laundromat. He put his coins in the slot. He could hear the ringing of the telephone, and then, much to his chagrin, he got the colonel's answering machine again!

"Colonel Whatley, this is agent Maroon 1, and I desperately need to talk to you. I have completed over seven missions in the past two years and am requesting a code red status update. I don't know how much longer I can hold out without getting paid and would like to discuss the retirement plan we had spoken about a few years ago. Extraction requested. Please respond by mail to my PO box with the checks for completing missions . . . all of them fatal . . . and if you can, please call me back at this number within the next half hour. I will be waiting for your reply. Maroon 1 out."

For an hour, he stayed and guarded the pay telephone at the laundromat. He carefully watched anyone that might be suspicious or a threat. For all of that Saturday morning, people cleaned their clothes, kept their eyes on their business, and refrained from making eye contact. They acted as though they were doing laundry. He knew better. He always did, and that was why he was still alive. Carefully, he shouldered his backpack and backed out of the laundromat. He could hear the distant sound of police sirens in the distance getting closer. Running up into the surrounding neighborhood, he found an empty dumpster and jumped inside. He knew that if the police had canine units, the scent of the trash could mask his smell. He heard what sounded like at least a half dozen patrol cars screech to a halt outside of the laundromat. They were searching for him on foot, and he could hear the sounds of dogs barking. After no more than a half an hour, they were gone.

***

Mayor Bill Black was pulling his hair out. In a city of just under one million residents, this shouldn't be happening. It was a city on edge. Residents were fearful to go to stores, merchants were calling for him to be removed, and he was sure to lose the next election unless somebody could catch the killer. For years, there had been horrific, gruesome homicides that had plagued the city, each with no apparent relation to each other. Innocent people from all walks of life were being found robbed and murdered, execution style. One was a night nurse with two children, another was a city lawyer and avid tennis player, yet another a garbage man with a family, then a store clerk going to night school, another a manicurist, then a pet groomer, and the latest victim an old optometrist. It was unfathomable. The only common thread between all of them was that they had been robbed after being killed and that nobody had survived to identify their attacker.

He had called the FBI in desperation. They had an ongoing six-month investigation that, quite frankly, had left much to be desired in terms of results. That is, until this morning. As part of a routine surveillance of phone calls emanating from the city, they had bugged the pay telephones and had come upon a call to a Colonel Whatley from a laundromat downtown. It was a strange enough call that it warranted a follow-up. What they found was astounding. Colonel Whatley had retired four years ago, and his phone had never been disconnected. For years, messages from a man calling himself Maroon 1 had accumulated on in the colonel's inbox—and all the messages were the ravings of a psychopath. In checking with the colonel, they found out the man had been discharged from the military for psychological delusions of grandeur. While in the care of hospital staff, for months, he had made no illusions about his being a counter-intelligence officer carrying out top-secret missions against enemies of the state. In truth, he was a private that had deep and disturbing mental issues that probably came from his tour of duty in Iraq. Eventually, he was released from the psychiatric ward, deemed mentally competent, and reintegrated back into society. In other words, he was honorably discharged.

***

An hour later, pushing the garbage off of his sleeve, he decided that it was time to get some answers. After paying for his bus fare with the money he had gotten from knocking off the head of the biggest crime family in town, he boarded the greyhound bus to the capitol. He smiled to himself and shook his head. How could anyone believe that the head of Cosa Nostra was an optometrist? Some people are just crazy. Well, it was time. He was ready to get his back pay. He wondered what Colonel Whatley would say when he showed up at his house in Virginia.

A Pirate's Affair

Dear Jack,

If you are reading this letter, then you have finally made it to Tortugas Beach. It is good that you are alive and well, and I hope you can take care of Elizabeth now. As you have probably noticed, there is no treasure left where we hid it, just this letter in its stead. Well, I will get right to the point. I have all of the jewels, gold and silver coins, and other assorted baubles that we captured from raiding the Spanish galleon—the San Vittorio—on our passage to the New World. I dug them up exactly six months and seven days after we buried them together. As for your fair share, you shall receive it in the body of this letter.

When we left England as friends and business partners, we agreed to split any treasure we each should encounter fifty-fifty and act like honorable men. Thus, when we happened to find the San Vittorio listing and crippled along the eastern seaboard of Florida, bereft of any crew, we knew it was wiser to hide the treasure than attract immediate attention. Granted, we each took a bit of the loot for extra spending money, but were careful not to take anything that may have been identified as being part of the ship's cargo or personal property.

Onward we traveled in high spirits, knowing that our dreams had been fulfilled. When we got to the Port of Kingston later that month to attend to the sugar cane business we had originally set out for, I thought nothing of having to leave you and my wife alone for a few months while I visited some of the neighboring islands to secure the proper rights and paperwork necessary for the business. It is during this time, I learned later, that you spent almost every day at our home, and even later, I learned that you began spending every night there as well.

Thus, when I returned to Kingston, with all of our business matters satisfactorily in hand, it was much to my surprise to be arrested and thrown in jail when I docked. Charged with sedition against the crown, I languished in a Port Royal jail cell for four months. I knew not who these charges came from at the time, but suffered immensely from the deprivations that come from being locked up in a tiny cell with two common criminals condemned to die. Later, of course, I learned through my lawyer that you were the person who had bribed the magistrate and had me arrested upon my return. Also, it had become common knowledge throughout the town that you had been spending freely, carousing in all of the brothels, all while keeping my wife content as well.

At this point, I guess you figured the story would end for me because you had paid a large enough bribe, as I later learned, to keep me incarcerated for years. As everyone knows, not many prisoners survive the rigors of being locked up on a tropical island. Luckily, I had not spent any of the extra loot that we had recently acquired, and with a few deeds to some sugar cane plantations we had agreed to purchase, I was able to buy my freedom from the very magistrate that had me locked up.

During my time in jail, I learned about all of the treacherous things you had done to betray me and of your plans to do away with me. In retrospect, it was the toughest time of my life, but it was also, in many respects, the most enlightening. The interminable, almost unbearable, solitude I felt led me down the path to many epiphanies about who I was and what I wanted out of my life. I had plenty of time to think clearly. And if I got my chance at freedom, I would cherish it with a new fondness.

My darling wife was no longer mine, nor did I want her back after how she so carelessly tossed me aside. And the more I thought about it, the more I felt sorry for the two of you. She was always a needy woman that needed trinkets to be satisfied, and I bet you obliged her, knowing what you would get in return. You bought yourself a young, unhappy woman who will never be satiated, like a siren calling from the rocks, and you will be obliged to carry yourself forth upon her shores. The problem, you may or may not have fully realized at this point, is that like a siren, once you go there, you are not allowed to leave and must listen to the wailing and shrieking for the rest of your life.

On the other hand, you always were the devious one, acting as though we were the best of brothers and part-ners until the time arose for you to strike, like a snake just waiting to uncoil and deal its deadly strike. When-ever you were short on cash, you had a plan to make some money with me and split it fifty-fifty. But now that I think back on it, I was the only one spending the money to outfit the expedition. If I guess correctly, the looted money that should have lasted you for a few years has probably slipped through your fingers as fast as the booze through your belly. Saving for the future was never one of your best attributes, and I can only guess that you soon started planning your trip back to Tortugas Beach with Elizabeth at your side.

But let me get to the point because you are soon-to-be a very busy man. When I left that jail cell, I promised myself to be rid of the two of you forever. I paid the mag-istrate not only for my freedom, but also promised him part of the treasure that I hid near where you are standing. To keep me safe, I didn't tell him exactly where I had it buried, but let him know that he should shadow you and

Elizabeth's movements and that the two of you would lead him to the island. I instructed him to lay in wait for the two of you to run out of money and then simply have you followed. He knows the directions to a small portion of the buried treasure from where you are currently standing. In fact, I bet if you look into the harbor at this very moment, you should see a crew of men coming ashore.

Finally, I left the magistrate some extra money for your seditious acts against the crown, which I chronicled prior to leaving for the treasure and England. At this very moment, I am most likely visiting your beloved youngest sister, Magdalena, and proposing that we venture out and see the world together. I do so very much find her to my liking. And please don't worry about Elizabeth too much because I hear the magistrate finds her quite attractive as well.

Give my sincerest regards to the men at Port Royal.

Richard

The Crow

The dark black crow cawed. Three times its voice carried above the din of the city, crying into the still night air. And for four successive times, it cawed three times. It was a message.

That was when the wind gusted, like it always did in the springtime, and thrust itself over the land, quieting everything in its path. The wind screamed and howled like a dirty madman before the silent stillness of the land returned.

And then the same crow spread its voice upon the wind three more times and called for its brethren. The call drove the crows to come and join him from wherever they were. From the trees, the wind, and the rooftops, each of them came.

In the twilight, the sky filled with black birds, long of wing and solid in flight. So easily they soared, responding to the call of fright that came right before the advent of the night. As usual, they were the first detectives to make it to the crime scene, circling and then dropping to the ground to make their customary inspection of the body. Nothing out of the ordinary. One to two caws bleated out, but the playground was not the usual place for death. But this wasn't a pretty town either. They knew the business; they were downtown crows.

The soft smells of juniper and alder drifted on the wind from fireplaces lit at the beginning of the evening. It melted into the bird's noses with the smell of fresh blood spilled across the gravel. It was a hearty, earthen smell that was a bit too sweet. Luckily, it was too cold and late for the ants who were below ground, unaware of the silent prize that lay above them.

The lead crow began to investigate the death. It was not a natural one at that. The victim was male, about 19, with short hair, old clothing, and few days' worth of stubble. The puddle of blood that surrounded his torso was a thick, congealing maroon-red mass. He had on blue jeans, an Oakland Raiders sweatshirt, and numerous tattoos on his left hand. He definitely looked the part of a gang member. Well, that is how it is. Easy come easy go.

They recognized the body. Of course, it was the new guy. Caw-caw-caw, one crow shouted out. This was the guy who sold small amounts of dope. This wasn't his neighborhood or territory, and the crows knew this, even if the victim didn't. This was Miguel's neighborhood. Lately, the new guy had been coming to the playground, encroaching on Miguel's turf, and the crows knew it, even if the new guy suspected nothing. They had seen it before, seen the consequences. Death was a simple matter to humans, especially Miguel.

It was a shame, but humans didn't value their lives like the crows did. How easy it was for the humans to kill or throw their lives away on drugs or eat themselves into obesity or stress themselves to death or smoke themselves into oblivion. It was the most remarkable of quirks found within nature. No other living creature would knowingly go against the laws of nature, except, that is, man. It was quite simply incredible. But the crows had stopped being amazed a long time ago. Based on their detailed observations, they knew that humans were deeply flawed, and for the most part, they kept their distance.

The police arrived shortly thereafter. Chalk was used to outline the body. Two detectives circled the body and cursorily looked around the surrounding area. Another man came up and took some notes, and soon, a few paramedics took the body away. The new guy was wheeled away on a gurney, all signs of him lost under a white sheet. The sheets weren't disposable like him: They could be washed clean. Two police officers talked about last week's poker game and the new blonde at the station with her humongous rack snugly tucked under her tight-fitting sweater. This punk got no love at all. It was a mundane death on a deserted basketball court. It was that simple. At least it was for the police.

The lead crow, one of the older, wiser ones in the group, was disgusted and incensed with the investigation. He had seen too many of these haphazard ridiculous excuses for an investigation over the years. He had liked the young man. Yes, he had been selling drugs, but the boy was poor and just trying to scratch out a meager existence on the hard streets. Just for some, like the boy, the streets encircled a little tighter than most others. The boy didn't have anyone he could call back on, an education, or even papers that made him legal. He didn't have a mother who could cope with life, no father in sight, and his only friend had been his imagination, and even that was often troubled. He had been alone trying to stay alive. And he always had been.

The detective picked up a rock and threw it in disgust. This was a dead-end case. Funds didn't exist in the budget to pursue a death like this. He had an inkling who committed the crime, but inklings didn't hold up in a court of law. They had spent enough money on the chalk outline. He turned to his partner and asked him if he wanted to go get a drink. It was the end of the day, and this was their third homicide of the day. Each of them saw the worst in humanity and, by the end of each day, their mouths were dry. It was enough to choke an elephant with a sunflower seed. His mouth was dry and dusty. You didn't need many excuses to get a drink after what they went through. No leads, no one talking, no clues, and no family members to help. It was an ugly business with ugly clientele. And to top it all off, it was always an ugly scene with dirty black birds that surrounded the perimeter, seemingly mocking them. God damn black crows with their cawing bullshit.

He turned and began walking away to the squad car when it hit him. At first, he thought he had been hit by a rock, but it was too soft for that, and then there was a tinkling sound as it smacked across the pavement. Startled, he watched as his partner reached toward the ground and picked up a necklace that had fallen from the sky! He recognized it at once. It was Miguel's, the local drug dealer, a long-time thorn in the police agency's side.

When they arrived at the ambulance to finish up the paperwork, he did a little more investigative work than usual. Pockets were turned inside out, and a few names on scraps of paper were revealed. There was a cell phone, and the detective decided he was going to track down some numbers and find out a bit more about who might have wanted this young man killed. He knew Miguel had done it once he saw the necklace. This was Miguel's signature piece of jewelry, an expensive piece of gold. The victim had most likely ripped it off of him in desperation.

He wanted to see Miguel pay for the crime. It was murder in the first degree as far as he was concerned. Funny how the evidence had been delivered to him from the sky, almost as if in an act of God.

As he got into his squad car, he glanced back at the playground. On the top of the school's flat roof, there was a crow looking directly at him, and it winked at him. Not once but twice. He couldn't believe it. Incredulously, he watched as the bird dove off of the roof and swooped toward his police car, and much like the amulet that had been dropped upon his head, it crapped directly in the middle of the police cruiser's windshield. It then flew away with one more backward glance as three caws sounded against the howl of the wind.

Manifest Destiny

Walking along the trails in the high desert region, Kevin enjoyed the feel of the cool air that surrounded him, the sun warming his shoulders and back. The crisp, fresh air cooled his nostrils, and occasionally, he would put his hand to his nose to give it a bit of warmth. The rays of the sun felt delicious as they drove deep inside his body, as though he was snuggled up next to his dog beside the fireplace. It was a wonderful Saturday morning, and this was his favorite time of the day. He had found a new trail to hike, one that went around the canyon that surrounded the dry arroyo, and he was engrossed in one of his favorite passions: rock collecting.

He could never get enough of it. Already that morning, he had found enough rocks to make one of his pockets bulge. He never tired of picking up the stones that lay strewn like jewels across the desert sands of the ancient lands of New Mexico. At home, he had thousands of rocks of all different colors and shapes he had collected from years of scouring the back trails, mountains, and valleys that surrounded his home. The rocks ranged in color from creamy whites to shiny yellows, translucent browns, and red flecked quartzes to white and gold-speckled pieces of granite. The individuality of each rock never ceased to inspire him. The area was a geological wonderland, being that it used to be underwater for millions of years prior to its present-day state. For the most part, the rocks were worn smooth from having been under the water for eons. They felt good to the touch, and it pleased him to place his hand in the pockets of his jacket, rubbing his newfound treasures.

The trail turned up, and looking west, he could see that the path wrapped around the hill. That would make for a nice hike because it would give him a good vantage point to see the valley below, which lay just on the other side of the hill. He climbed slowly, enjoying the sunlight that warmed his back. It was a cloudless morning, save for a few remaining cumulous clouds from the previous evening's rain. They were white oases, hiding princesses in castles and unicorns within deep forests, drifting among a deep cobalt blue sky that seemingly stretched to infinity. He thought of the afternoons and late evenings when the sky would change to bright pinks, orange hues, and purple maroon magentas. At other times, the sky would tower with thunder boomers that bespoke of the power of the gods as they beat upon their drums. The best mornings were just like this, a peaceful rich blue sky above, almost like an ocean that lay above him, where birds flew through the seas of the air.

Kevin listened to the crows and how they differentiated themselves, each with their own particular cawing. He labeled them this way. The one he was listening to was a three-caw crow—it seemed to be jawboning with a four-caw crow that was farther up the side of the hill. He wondered if, based upon their cawing pattern, each of them had their own status in crow society. It must be, he thought. He once heard a one-caw crow and that was about as rare as stumbling on a five-caw crow. Immersed in his own thoughts about the crows, he reached the summit and gazed down on the other side. The trail stretched out in front of him, and he could see that it appeared to loop through some Ponderosa pines as it descended. Searching his hand through the front pocket of his jeans, he found a hard watermelon candy and popped it into his dry mouth. The flavor filled his mouth, and the instant sugar rush lifted his spirits.

Passing through the pines, he caught sight of a rabbit that had not noticed him yet. It was one of those big hares with ears that extended almost a foot from their heads, a black-tailed jackrabbit. He just stared and watched the rabbit as it foraged for food among the cactus and rocks that littered the old Permian seashore. He noticed that its nose twitched and saw that its small black eye caught sight of him. The rabbit was gone in an instant, scampering far away into the bushes. A feeling of satisfaction reached him, knowing that he had crept up on the animal and had been able to view it without it recognizing his presence.

He continued his trek along the path. In vain, he attempted to catch sight of the rabbit again. Shading his eyes, he scanned about fifty feet away. That was when the glint of something caught his eye. It was shiny and reflected the sunlight in a strange sort of way. Probably someone's discarded beer or soda can, but as long as he was here, he decided to stray away from the trail and investigate. Cautiously, he made his way around the prickly pear and other cactuses to where the object lay. The closer he got, the more it began to intrigue him. Reaching down, he picked the object off of the desert floor and turned the wondrous thing around and around within his hands. It was magnificent.

The object fit nicely in the palm of his hand and appeared to be completely encased within a half an inch of translucent amber. He had never seen anything like it in his life. He had seen animals encased in amber when he had visited a natural history museum, but this object appeared to be man-made! It was a few inches in length and an inch wide and faintly reminded him of a horseshoe crab. It was silver in color, and running lengthwise, it had red circular dots along one side of its outer shell. At the end of the object was a needle like tail with a circular nodule at the tip. For more than five minutes, he gazed and guessed at what the fantastic object was before finally placing it in his jacket.

By the time he got back home, he was out of breath. He had run the last mile as fast as his legs could carry him, the excitement from wanting to show his parents the object being too much. His parents were sitting at the breakfast table reading the newspaper when he ran inside the house and produced the object from his pocket. Each of them looked it over and exclaimed how different and unusual it was, but not much more was said about it— his mom went back to eating her breakfast, and his father resumed reading his newspaper. A bit disappointed in their lack of enthusiasm, he took the object to his room and looked at it for a while before he noticed his fish tank. It would be the perfect place to keep his newest treasure, and he dropped it in his fish tank and watched it settle on the bottom.

Unbeknownst to him, stasis had been destroyed. The first bubble, almost unnoticeable, slipped up from the object, floating past a goldfish that paused before swimming on. The beacon had been activated. A signal emanating from the tail began transmitting, while a faint red, pulsing light flashed along the one side of the object. Slowly, the amber coating, which wasn't really amber at all, disintegrated. The red circular lights that ran lengthwise began to light up and flash in different patterns. Thousands of microscopic multi-celled organisms burst forth from the probe. To the visible eye, nothing was happening, but on a subatomic molecular level, the water was being filled with the building blocks of an alien life form unknown to man.

The fish swimming in the tank felt it first. Hundreds and then thousands of the microscopic organisms began coating the outsides of the two fish. Within minutes, their gills were closed, and their mouths were filled with a substance that could only be described as a creamy yellow glue. Soon enough, the fish were dead, unable to breathe. For the next few hours, the microorganisms fed upon the two floating carcasses until the skeletons drifted to the bottom of the tank. The small white backbones stood out against the pink and blue coral stones that lay at the bottom of the tank. Within the next few hours, the tank was cleaned of all the algae and any other carbon-based form of life.

Hurtling across space, the signal had been transmitted utilizing a high-frequency spectrum monitored by the Galatians. Even though the signal was relatively weak, the frequency was monitored with high-powered amplification equipment, which enabled them to track down its origin. And even though the Galatians were over two parsecs from this unknown galaxy, they would be able to pick up the signal within a month. Once the signal was received, it was only a matter of time before the earth would have visitors. They desperately needed to colonize a planet that had abundant water and, knowing that the beacon would not have been activated unless the casing had been dissolved in water, they were sure to come. In their search for a suitable planet, thousands of the probes had been sent in all directions across the universe with the hope that, someday, they would receive a signal. That day would arrive in exactly twenty-nine days, seven hours, and thirty-four minutes, after the Galatians had waited for over two hundred and forty-eight years.

The silicon-based organism interspersed itself evenly throughout the fish tank. When the strainer came into the tank and fished out the two carcasses, they clung to it, invisible to the naked eye. When the strainer touched the toilet water, they found a whole new breeding ground and began reproducing at an astronomical rate. When introduced by accident from the mother's hand to her mouth and then to her son and husband with kisses goodnight, it was a fatal passing of the organism that led to their final dreams. Dreams of drowning and suffocation clouded all of their minds until they succumbed to the organisms and never woke up.

But it was no dream. In the afternoon the police showed up, alerted by concerned relatives and acquaintances that none of them had shown up to work or school and that nobody was able to contact them. What they found were three dead bodies with their nostrils and mouths filled with a gluey yellowish fluid. Not understanding the seriousness of the situation, the police, paramedics, and coroner all failed to treat the situation with proper care. With the water system of the town and the Rio Grande River infected, as well as all the first responders to the scene, the Galatian epidemic had begun.

The speed with which the silicon-based organism spread was frightening. People taking showers, washing dishes, having a cool ice-filled drink all became infected within minutes and spread it to others. With the power to double every seven seconds, the organism was in control of a territory of over one hundred square miles before the authorities at the Centers for Disease Control were even notified a day later that something was amiss. Within three days, the whole state of New Mexico was under quarantine, but it was ineffectual. The organism was designed to keep eating, multiplying, and spreading. It traveled along waterways and plumbing systems and by the way of infected people fleeing for their lives. From Santa Fe to the mouth of the Rio Grande, it pushed outward in all directions, spreading like an uncontrolled wildfire. The fish carried it northward to Colorado, to the fish-eating bear in Durango, while people half crazed with fear drove it to the deserts of Arizona and the plains of Texas. Soon news reports were spreading that all the waters of the Gulf of Mexico to the Atlantic Ocean were contaminated. Blockades and quarantines could not stop the virulent spread of the organism. The cost of bottled water dated prior to the epidemic was worth more than the price of gold. Chaos reigned across the globe. It was the beginning of a pandemic in which no human or animal, no matter how remote, was spared.

In retrospect, the Galatian epidemic should have been foreseen. A planet with such vast quantities of clean water was the most valuable prize in the universe. And a planet that was self-sustaining was truly a miracle throughout the multitude of galaxies. When the Galatians arrived, they stayed on the edge of the atmosphere. Painstakingly, they scanned, recorded, and analyzed all the data from the planet. Their scans indicated that the planet had been cleared of all previous animal life forms that may have either proved hostile or dangerous to their colonization. And as a bonus, over fifty percent of the plant's species would survive. It was time to introduce the antidote to the silicon-based organism. Probes filled with the antidote were jettisoned to different sections of the planet, and upon contact with water, released a counter to the organism. It would take another two weeks for the cleansing of the planet to be completed by the carbon-based organism. In turn, this new mutant-based carbon organism, which fed solely on the silicon-based organisms, would be extinct a week after exterminating its food source. It was a clean, efficient process of sterilizing the planet prior to colonization.

In the following months, the Galatians marveled at the structures that were present upon the planet, both natural and those made by the previous inhabitants. There was no empathy felt for those that they had conquered because it was their manifest destiny and international right under the laws of Galatia to conquer and live wherever they desired. There was a profound lack of sympathy for all the species they caused to become extinct. Their own survival was paramount to all other concerns. They were pleased with themselves and ecstatic to have located a water-rich planet that they could conform to their own desires. After eking out an existence on a dying planet for thousands of years, devoid of any sustainable water sources, they were able to appreciate having colonized such a bountiful planet.

Unfortunately for the Galatians, they failed to realize that in a few select underground caverns, deep below the surface of the planet, some of the previous inhabitants had survived and were working on a plan to take back their planet. The fight for the planet and its natural resources had only just begun.

A Turn of Events

My life changed so fast. I had been minding my own business in the restroom of Grumwalt's discount store when one man mutilated and killed another man right in front of me. A mulatto man, full of muscle with a medium build, had been the last one to enter. He casually approached the two of us as we faced the urinals set along the wall. I don't think I even got a good look at his face. Suddenly, with all of his strength, he swung his fist in a roundhouse motion and split open the other man's mouth as he was peeing at a urinal next to me. I could hear the sound of teeth pinging into the urine-soaked floor, intermixed and mingled with the happy elevator music chimed throughout the store. Instantly, a geyser of blood hemorrhaged out of the man's mouth. In the next moment, his attacker, wearing a tight gray windbreaker that wrapped around his bulging arms, proceeded to ram the man's face into the tile wall. I can still remember the sound of the cartilage crunching and bones snapping. The helpless victim, with his pants around his ankles, was a shattered mess within seconds, and his screams were a gurgled mess of surprise, pain, and horror. Somehow, he already knew this was the end for him.

Blood had splattered across my dick, underwear, pants, and shirt. Aghast at the assault, all I could do was try and get away from the scene as fast as possible. The problem was my private member didn't know any better and was still pissing. There was no hope for this man next to me, and I had no idea if I was going to be next because I was a witness to this brutal crime. I knew a professional hit man when I saw one. Zipping up my pants, my dick still pissing, I got it caught in the zipper, pinching it, yet I couldn't have cared less. By the time I had backed away a few steps and zipped up, the man next to me was on the ground and getting kicked in the head by enormous black military boots. The boots crashed into the victim's ears, cheeks, and what remained of the man's mouth. I could hear the store alarm intermittently going off in the distance in between the sounds of a jazz trumpeter.

By this time, and all of this happened within seconds, the man on the ground was knocked out cold, and the hulking man pulled out a knife and stuffed it between the man's ribs and began twisting. He obviously was sending some type of message to the soon-to-be deceased man's family. The thought went through my mind that this man had crossed one of the underworld crime syndicates and owed them money. The body began involuntarily jerking to the awful screeching sounds that the man made through his smashed face, and then, the muscled man pulled the knife from the ribs and, with his other hand, pulled up the man's head by his hair while pinning the man's arms down with his knees and delicately put the knife under his neck and deeply cut into him, slashing open the windpipe and jugular vein in one quick motion.

Watching it all, my eyes bulging out of their sockets, I came to my senses and bolted for the door. In total, it had been less than a minute since this whole awful nightmare had begun. Unbeknownst to me, my problems had just started. The first problem was that I was witness to a murder. And I might be next. I could feel the left eye of the murderer follow my movement from his crouched position as he finished up cutting the man's neck. Not daring to look back, I thrust the door open as the store alarm blared in my ears, so much louder now that I was out of the bathroom. I noticed the store cameras following my movements as I dashed through the aisles. I didn't even consider that I could possibly be named a suspect—I just fled for my life, splattered in blood, through the store aisles and out the exit. I remember at one point that I turned around to see if he was following me, but I didn't see the man in the windbreaker. That is, until later that evening.

***

At home that night, looking at my personalized weekly news for the benefit of the state, I happened to catch a video clip of myself running through the store. Afterward, the man in the gray windbreaker was talking to the newswoman, in tears no less, going on about how he witnessed the whole thing. He told her that I had killed the man and fled the bathroom! The newswoman was asking for help with identifying who I was. I was a wanted man for murder. Once I was caught, guilty or not, because everyone was always guilty once they made the news, my mind would be cleansed, and I would be sent to the work rehabilitation program out in the badlands for the rest of my existence. It was a death sentence.

I didn't have a lot of time before the facial recognition software that the Terran forces used would shut down my credit. Drones would be alerted to my Terran identification number, and at every street corner, alarms would blare. I had seen it happen to others, and nobody got more than a few street corners away before they were either surrendered or blasted into gel. I needed to get access to as many credits as fast as possible without alerting any suspicion from the state, all while attempting to gain access to the black network that supposedly survived outside the major cities. At least, these were the rumors I had heard.

I gave myself a few moments to try and calm down and get in the correct state of mind. Then, I switched on my personal assistant of the state.

"Hi, John, how are you this evening?" the sweet voice of treachery sang out to me.

"I am great Lucy. I think I might have found a mate on my own!"

"Oh John, that is great news. But don't you think that might be a little too risky with your diagnosed level three bipolar disorder and level four dysfunctional family history?" she cooed at me with so much false concern.

"No, I don't believe so Lucy . . . I really feel that this woman could be a suitable match for me and the state. She is a little bit shy, very intelligent, and has level five dependency issues that match perfectly with my level three control issues. I met her today at a coffee shop, and after a few hours, we agreed to try a controlled rendezvous at the OASIS on Verna Five, that is, if the state will allow it. I have been saving a few credits just in case something like this ever happened and really would like you to approve, if you could, Lucy? Her name is Liz Diamond identification 300059813. I know things haven't worked out so well with the state matches recently, but I believe I might just have found a suitable mating partner. Just imagine how many level four analysts she might be able to conceive for the state if you approved."

I dangled the carrot out there for Lucy, my state-sponsored computer life assister, on recorded lines without going overboard and arousing any suspicion. The woman I had chosen was Liz Diamond. I worked with Liz Diamond, a state librarian, for the past five years, but only on a completely professional level. She wasn't my type, but I couldn't think of anyone else that I knew of and an identification number. Typically, they did not approve of releasing credits for matches not set up by the state, but I had mentioned that I would be using one of their controlled platforms for the meeting, Verna Five, and recently, my state matches had been an abysmal failure. I could almost hear the time click away as the state analyzed my request, the pros and cons, and if they would release my credits. After a minute's time, Lucy was back on the line.

"Hi, John. I have good news for you. Now, ordinarily, we would not approve of such a rendezvous, but there is an outside phase two polarity that this match could actually work. We tabulated the results from the psychological sequencer on both of your biomes and have approved the request. How many credits would you like released?"

"That is great news, Lucy. I really feel like this is the one for me. I would like to make this trip special, and because I have overtime scheduled for the next six months, I would like to request all of my available credits be released, if that is ok with the state?"

There was a thirty second pause before Lucy spoke.

"John, the state has authorized you eleven credits. We can't authorize your full savings account because that would not be in the state's best interest or yours. One must be prudent you know."

I could hear the fake laughter of Lucy on the other end of my personal assistant, and I swore under my breath. A God damn computer was laughing at me.

"Oh, I am sure the eleven will be fine. Thank you so much Lucy for all your help. Prudence is a good thing."

"Oh, it has been my pleasure serving you, John. Have a wonderful time with Liz Diamond on Verna Five. Goodbye."

Turning the personal assistant off, I breathed a sigh of relief. The good news was that the Terran forces had not yet actualized my facial recognition yet, and I was able to pull most of the credits I had amassed over my many years of overtime. Still, though, they had not given me everything I had asked for. I was going to have to forfeit the remaining nine credits once I left the state, if I got that far. The state was always protective over its own interest's above that of the individual. I guessed that they released as many credits as they did because I let them know I was going to use their OASIS platform.

They were going to profit from my vacation—coworkers had said the prices were exorbitant.

Flinging off my blue blood-stained one-piece worker suit and white walking shoes, I proceeded to immerse myself in cleansing gel and then towel off. If I was lucky enough to escape the state's perimeter, it would be the last time I ever would need to do that again. Anxious, but feeling slightly refreshed, I began gathering everything I needed.

***

First, I found my credits waiting for me, and rather than putting them on my credit account stored in my arm tabulator, I had them delivered to me physically. The eleven credits were disk shaped and fit nicely within the palm of my hand. In this way, they could not shut down the access to my arm tabulator once they established I was a wanted fugitive. I was attempting to think a few steps ahead of every move the state was bound to make. The next thing I did was kiss my cat goodbye right before I dropped it down the rescue shoot. It would end up in someone else's apartment within a few hours or a few days, or it would be put down if nobody claimed it. A twinge of pain and remorse tugged at my heart for disposing of my only companion for the past five years, but it was better than to have it caught by the Terran forces when they eventually raided my home. I had heard stories about their cruelty to all living things and would rather see it alive and happy with someone else than a pile of goo.

I grabbed my gun, drone net, face hologram, hoodie, survival kit, and a few changes of outfits. I took just enough to fit inside a backpack and duffle bag. I would have to catch a ride because I knew once I had been identified, my vehicle would be shut off. It was time. I looked in the mirror. I knew I was kidding myself. It was only a matter of time before they caught me. My chances of escaping to the off-world were slim to none, statistically speaking. And I knew the statistics since that was part of my state job. What I was attempting was insanity. Most would argue that I should just go to the police and that they would understand that I was not the killer. Justice would prevail.

***

But I knew how things operated within the state. The state had clandestine agreements with crime syndicates because they paid the state kickbacks, and all the state wanted was a fall guy so that they could trump up their crime-fighting statistics and make a martyr out of me. I was dispensable and disposable. My mundane job was a statistical analyst for the state. I knew how they crunched numbers and looked for arrests that could corroborate with crimes, regardless if the man or woman convicted was actually guilty. That was irrelevant to the state. The state needed to keep its high conviction rate to justify the taxes on its citizenry. It was the trade-off. My only chance, slim as it might be, was that I knew how the system worked in many respects, and that gave me a slight edge. It was a good thing I had accumulated some of the underground weaponry, like the drone net and face hologram, over the past years.

I grabbed a ride at the end of the street just after using my face hologram.

"Where to buddy?" said the middle-aged man, who I guessed was of Pakistani descent by his accent and look.

"I want to go to Landower Falls."

"Whoa, wait a second, for that kind of trip, I am going to have to see a half a credit, in advance."

Not wanting to pay for the trip with my eleven credits, but rather with my reserve that the state still held, I nervously placed my arm with my palm face up under the driver's scanner. It identified that I had enough for at least a half a credit, and the driver was satisfied.

"Well it looks like you are going for a long hike, huh?" he said in a half friendly, but also inquisitive, almost suspicious way, glancing at my gear.

I didn't feel much like talking and needed him to get me there fast.

"Yes, I am a photographer, and the light is just perfect this time of day for my shoots. If you can get me there in under a half hour, I will give you an extra tenth credit. It is seven o'clock right now. The lighting will be perfect then, but unfortunately, it takes me a little while to set up the camera equipment."

"Wow! You got it buddy. That will make my day."

He sped up and forgot about me for a while, with his mind intent on driving. I could tell he desperately wanted to get the extra tenth of a credit. Times were tight for everyone.

Crackling over the car antennae, the state news began with its top story.

"Insurgent forces were stopped from entering the state on the western border, and seventeen of them were killed in a firefight. Another five were captured as prisoners and will be cleansed to work in the high desert mines. It was another successful operation with only minimal losses. Two Terran force members were wounded, and one was captured. Our other top story of the night came from the downtown area where a man was viciously murdered at Grumwalt's department store. At this time, we have identified his attacker as John Savage and are asking for your help in apprehending this dangerous criminal, whose identification number is 600045355. As always, there is a five-credit reward for any information that leads to the criminal's capture."

Across the screen, my face flashed, and I noticed the driver look down to see the face. It was a good thing that my face was distorted from the hologram program I was using.

"What did you say your name was again?" asked the driver.

"I didn't. My name is Steve Pollack. Are we almost there yet? The shadows are getting long, and I don't want to miss my shots."

"Oh, yes. We are just about five minutes away, and we will be just under thirty minutes, so I'll be expecting that extra tenth of a credit you promised."

"Oh, good."

With the driver's attention focused back on the traffic ahead of him, and on that extra tenth of a credit, he failed to realize the drone that had been following us for the past mile. It was flashing, bobbing, and weaving, attempting to get the numbers on the car so that it could send in an alert to the state to have the car stopped with automatic shut off. The driver turned the next corner.

Moving up close behind him, I shoved a grade eight relaxant needle into his neck. It was all he could do to turn and look at me, eyes wide open with surprise, before he slumped across the front seat. With no pressure being applied to the accelerator, I grabbed the wheel of the car and moved it toward the curb. It would hit another car in about five seconds as it slowly decelerated, which was just enough time for me to jump out of the back seat with my bags and roll over on to the sidewalk.

My shoulder slammed into the pavement as I hit the ground, but I was out of the taxi with a few seconds to spare. The car, although visibly slowing down, was still traveling at about twenty miles an hour when it crashed into a parked car, just as the drone turned the corner. The drone, thirty feet up in the air and still flashing its lights, stopped just behind the car with its cameras working the area. Out of my duffle bag, I pulled my drone net and launched it before the camera had swept me. The net encircled the drone, and I quickly tied it off to the pole of a streetlight. I wasn't sure if its cameras had caught my actions prior to me running for my life. The running was difficult with both the duffle bag and backpack, but it was all I could do to get away. Already, a few pedestrians were starting to gather at the scene of the accident and were pointing in my direction.

I could hear the wail of sirens getting closer. The Terran state forces were just too efficient for anyone, including myself, to escape. Even with knowledge of their tactics, I felt doomed: in the end, my mind would be cleansed. The police airships would be there momentarily. The trap was closing. And fast.

Landower Falls was still over a mile away, and even if I got there, it was manned by state guards. My original plan was to make some type of diversion with a kerosene lamp I had stuffed in my survival pack, but with them knowing I was in the area, the hope of catching them by surprise had vanished. I didn't have much time to think things over when I made my escape plan, and the futility of my present situation was becoming all too evident. My arm started throbbing. It was coming. I was terrified. They had found my identification number and were obviously very close to capturing me. They had a tracker pulsing my arm. The drone had been able to capture my identification prior to me having tied it off. My arm began to feel very heavy, like a stone was attached to my wrist, and then, my arm began speaking to me.

"Give up now, John Savage. We have your identification number. We know you are trying to escape, but your actions are futile. We have you surrounded. Stop what you are doing and wait for our agents to pick you up. Justice will be served. Everyone is innocent until proven guilty in accordance with our state laws."

The message kept repeating itself as my arm started flashing in an array of colors; then, it began to let out a siren's wail as I turned the corner. In front of me was an alley in the old section of town, built prior to the secular riots of 2140 when the people had revolted against the state. I was trapped, but I wasn't ready to give up just yet. Running down the alley, my legs felt like cinder blocks.

"Trying to run away from our rendezvous?"

In front of me, in a cream-colored one-piece pantsuit and with her arms crossed, was Liz Diamond. I stopped in my tracks.

"Wh–wha–", I panted, "Are you doing here?"

"I figured you were in trouble. I received a confirmation notice about our rendezvous on Verna Five right after I saw your picture on the news for murdering a man in a bathroom. I mean, I just couldn't let a catch like you go after hearing about how you treat people, so I tailed you from your apartment. When I arrived at your apartment, I saw you leaving. But right now, that isn't important. Here, put this on over your arm and fast." It was a charcoal sleeve of some sort that went up to my elbow. Immediately, the flashing and the sound of the siren stopped. "Now, pick up that manhole cover in the alley and push it to the side. Quickly, you only have a few seconds before they arrive."

I did as she said. I was not completely comprehending what was happening, but knew that in some way, she was trying to help and protect me. She had a funny, almost smug look on her face. She obviously was in more control of the situation than I was. The sleeve fit snugly over my arm, and miraculously, it blocked the signal from the state. My arm stopped throbbing. Straining with all of the strength left in my body, I barely got the manhole cover raised up off the level of the street—the cockroaches hidden beneath it scattered away from the movement and light. I turned around and saw her entering into the alley wall! It was a hidden entrance through a brick wall she had opened by pulling on an old wire dangling from an electrical conduit that ran down the side of the building. I followed her. And just in time too! I could hear boot steps on the other side of the wall that stopped right where the manhole cover had been dislodged. The manhole cover being pulled up was a diversion she had instructed me to make.

We walked in silence, mainly because I was out of breath and scared that the Terran forces would hear me. We went down a long, dim corridor for at least a hundred feet before the passage turned to the right and some stairs came. She went up, and I followed.

"Leave your bags at the bottom of the steps. You are too conspicuous carrying them."

I did as she ordered. Still, this was crazy. She was the librarian at the state statistical headquarters who I only casually flirted with to get my job done. It wasn't that she was bad looking, in fact, quite the opposite. In a strange sort of way, she was beautiful, but I never imagined her as anything more than a studious librarian and a staunch party member. Now, I was taking orders from her to escape from the state.

She looked through a peep hole at the top of the stairs, moved her hand across some sort of latch, and then opened the door. Our next step was onto the top of a sink inside of a restroom. She adeptly hopped down from the sink counter and looked up at me with a slight smirk. I got down from the counter and watched as she swung the door above the bathroom sink closed, which was concealed by a huge mirror. She let me know that I should probably clean myself up before entering the coffee house because I was looking a bit disheveled. I was dripping from head to toe with sweat. I readily agreed and took a few minutes to clean myself up, all while attempting to regain my composure.

"So, Ms. Liz Diamond, just who are you? And why did you decide to save me? I mean, it is not often that a man makes a rendezvous with a woman behind her back, is accused of murder, and gets saved by his date who was only notified by the state as a precautionary measure."

She flashed me a look that bordered between understanding and concern.

"You, Mr. Savage, are in deep trouble. The state has its priorities, and they mean to arrest you, cleanse your mind, and have you work for free for them for the rest of your life, all in blissful ignorance."

At this, she smiled at me, a nice pretty smile with raised eyebrows that showed she knew the danger I was caught up in.

"Furthermore, you have gotten me in a bit of trouble by using me as your alibi to access your credits. Shame on you. But I do understand that sometimes things happen beyond our control and that you were in a bit of a sticky situation at that moment. I helped you, not only because I like you and pity you, but I detest the machinations of the unholy state that society currently finds itself trapped by. I am part of the underground that ferries those unfortunate souls that get on the state's bad side, be it by their own means or just bad luck. In your case, after knowing you for years, I can't imagine you committing that horrible murder. Plus, I recognized the tearjerking thug on the state program as a known syndicate member. It is part of my job to know such things."

She paused and sighed and continued, "So by sheer dumb luck, you got into this whole mess by pissing at the wrong spot and at the wrong time. Then by, I would almost say, providential good luck, you summoned me for a date on Verna Five. I can provide you that escape that you so desperately need, but not exactly to an oasis like Verna Five. I will get you off the city grid and get you in contact with members of the off-the-grid network. Your new life begins now. You will undergo an operation to remove the identification tracker in your arm once you are out of the city. You will live with the help of others, like yourself, and learn to depend upon them, yourself, and the survival skills you learn. But you will be free from the state. No longer will you be a cowering, convalescent ward. If you survive, you will become a real man and, I suspect, a valuable member of the resistance."

At this, she looked wistfully at me like I was the one who was the lucky one in this arrangement of exile. Maybe I was. We walked through the coffee shop, and I saw her wink at the owner, who nodded his head at her.

A day later, I was fifty miles from the outskirts of the city with my backpack and duffle bag, walking up a trail toward an off-the-grid outpost. I was told they could help me on my new journey. I still wore my sleeve to cover my identification tracker. They would help with that as well. As I trudged up the dusty trail, it was all that I could do to try and stop thinking about how much I would have liked to have gone on that trip with Liz Diamond, or whoever she was, to Verna Five for a rendezvous.

The Legend of Mi-Way-To

Desperately looking for calm within the storm, the waters rushed, tumbled, and crashed over the jagged rocks and boulders that sat high up in the mountains of the Gods. With a turgid recklessness, the waters raced over moss-encrusted stones, crashing into trees along the banks of the rivers, sometimes ripping them from their safe havens and tossing the behemoths about like tiny bits of flotsam. It was approaching winter, and the late rains had begun in earnest upon the sacred land of the Oglala. It had rained for eight straight days and nights, and the river at the bottom of the mountains was swollen tight like a female buffalo in her last month of gestation. The rains were a precursor to winter and also the annual raiding of their village by their enemies, the Lakota. It was time for the high council to convene and for the ceremony of the passing of the seasons to be held. Unlike in years past, when times were good, this year might decide the fate of the tribe, which had been decimated from five years of losses to the Lakota. The tribe was faltering, and everyone within the tribe was all too aware of their precarious situation.

For five successive years, the Lakota had raided their lands, stolen the crops they had stored up for the long winters, killed many of their braves, and captured and enslaved the best of their young women to serve as their warriors' mistresses. Many of the elders had starved in the winters because of not having enough crops to eat. Too many of their young men had been killed in battle and were not around for the hunting season when the tribe needed them. Without fertile women to bring new blood into the world and young men to feed the tribe, the future was looking bleak for all of them. People were beginning to whisper that the buzzards were starting to circle the tribe. So when the life-giving rains came after the harvests had been sown and reaped, it was with a cruel irony that the members of the village began to fear for their futures, instead of rejoicing in the rains that restored their land with life.

As the sun set over the horizon and played shadow games over the huts, all of the adult members of the tribe gathered at the center of the village, just along the banks of the swollen river. A roaring fire had been built with tree limbs as thick as legs placed in a tri-pod fashion, a sign that everyone expected the meeting would last deep into the night. Mi-Way-To, the chief's youngest son, was present to keep the fire going throughout the night, or otherwise, he would have been off with the other children of the village, being tended to by the medicine woman, La-Shi-Na. Tonight, as was customary, the elders would decide the fate of the tribe. The aged chief, Oh-Wat-Tu, would preside over the gathering and would come to the final decision about what his people should do after hearing from all those who spoke.

The chief's second oldest son, leader of the tribal hunts and chief among the warriors, spoke first. He spoke of how they could defend their village and beat the enemy, even though they were outnumbered by almost three to one. He spoke of the bravery of the Oglala people, its warriors of the past, and the great triumphs in their history and of a plan where everyone would have to learn to fight and defend themselves, including the women, children, and elderly. He stressed the sacrifices that they would have to endure to ensure their safety and the tribe's survival.

The chief's oldest son spoke next. He had lost two of his sons over the past few years and could plainly see how the successive wars had weakened the tribe, so he proposed a different plan of action. He spoke of appeasement. Let them give gifts of their food and a few of their squaws, as well as some of their young braves, in place of fighting rather than losing them in battle. He felt that the tribe could not handle another loss of young men, and it was better to give some rather than have all of what they owned taken away. Many of the tribe did not like the thought of giving anything to their sworn enemy, but there was some wisdom in his words because the odds were against them in battle, and it might bide them the time they needed until they could recoup their strength.

The third son spoke of leaving their ancestral land. If they left, he rationalized, they would neither lose their crops, women, nor their lives, but they could find themselves a better place to live out west. And if they ever did become strong again in numbers and force, they could move back and recapture the land they had left behind. He let them know that it was folly to try and wage war against a clearly superior force in open battle, and to give gifts to the other tribe was to sleep with the dark spirit that lived in the mountain.

Within each of the three proposals, there was logic, and the people of the Oglala tribe debated for hours among themselves while Mi-Way-To, the youngest of the chief's sons, tended and fed the fire, all the while listening to each of the conversations. Finally, the chief, with long ridges and lines running up and down his face like the small tributaries that crossed the land, asked if there were any other proposals that the tribe should consider. The gathering was silent in deference to the chief's sons' proposals. That is, until a small voice could be heard clearing his throat. Most of the villagers were shocked to hear Mi-Way-To speak. It was known throughout the tribe that he had been horribly afflicted by the loss of his grandfather during the first Lakota raid five years ago and had fallen silent for many years. The people all turned and stared at him.

The boy spoke, "If we are to survive and live where we rightfully belong and crush our enemies, then we must be sly like the fox, as powerful as the bear, and as crafty as the owl. We must harness the great spirits of the earth, the sun, and the rain and make them our friends in this battle. We must take advantage of our enemies' weaknesses and vanity while appealing to their greed and hunger for war against a weaker opponent. We must utilize our ancestor's cunning and skill in the ways of fighting and maybe even a few of them as they are today? We need to fight and finish them before they finish off our tribe!" Then, the young man laid out his plan to all of the tribe.

Ten days after the rains stopped, the Lakota readied themselves for battle. Confident in their upcoming victory and greedy for the spoils of war, they rode their horses to the top of a hill that looked over the Oglala village. Everything looked in order. There was a roaring fire in the center of the village by the river, which was next to the storehouse filled with meats and grains, and surrounding the fire were five squaws cooking the tribes evening meal, their backs turned to them. The women had long black hair that extended down their backs and were wearing brightly colored shawls. A few of the braves on top of the hill, laughing, began picking out which one they wanted once the wampum was over.

Yelling their war cries, they charged down the hillside. Immediately, they could see some of the villagers scattering into the surrounding brush that encircled their encampment. This was going to be easier than they had imagined. The women were still tending to the fire, oblivious to the impending attack. The braves felt pleased with themselves and yelled even louder as they galloped unopposed into the center of the village. Jumping down from his horse, the chief of the Lakota tried to spin around one of the women tending to the fire and got the shock of his life. In front of him stood five skeletons, all covered in shawls, each with a wig of long black hair. The braves were so surprised and confused, they failed to notice that a few of the Oglala were on the banks of the river, both to the north and south of them, and some others were encircling the village. They were taking out what seemed to be large wooden platforms made of trees that were bound together. These had been placed at the edges of the river vertically to hold back the water, while at a few places surrounding the village, they had been placed horizontally where the braves had crossed to get to the village's center. As the platforms near the water's edge came up, the water from the swollen river instantly filled the empty void. In less than a minute, and well before the Lakota could stop the Oglala, they found themselves surrounded by a ten foot wide and ten foot deep moat that had been dug prior to their arrival. It was a trap!

The Lakota soon gathered their senses but quickly realized that the Oglala had set up defensive positions all along the outside of the village and had encircled them on three sides, with the swiftly moving river on the fourth side blocking them off. That was when one of the braves called out from the storehouse. Moving in unison to the storehouse, they stopped at the door and found it was cleared out of any food, save for a rancid rotting deer carcass filled with maggots and covered in flies. In each successive hut, they found the same rotting piece of meat waiting for them. And then the men began to scratch themselves, realizing that fleas had been left in the village. Enraged, one of the stronger braves tried to fjord the deep moat that stood between them and freedom. The horse fell off the side of the steep embankment and directly into the water, bucked its rider, and not being able to get back on land, he was picked up downstream by the Oglala. It was a disaster. The Lakota warrior, angry with being bucked, crawled back on land and stood up. At that moment, an arrow pierced his heart, and his final cry rang out among them. Soon, arrows were thick in the air. The massacre had begun.

With nowhere to hide except the storehouse, they retreated to the safety of its walls while they regrouped and tried to come up with a plan. The Oglala were not going to give them a chance. The roof and ceiling of the storehouse had been stuffed with highly flammable dry grass, and once the Lakota were inside, flaming arrows began to hit the roof. Within minutes, the building was ablaze, and the Oglala had taken up even better positions so that when the Lakota came rushing out of the burning building, they were shot down on the spot. In less than an hour, the battle was over. Not one Lakota warrior remained, and not one Oglala villager had been injured.

Afterward, the Oglala celebrated their victory, gathered up their new stock of prize horses, and made a journey to the land of the Lakota, taking back all their women who had been stolen over the past years. Grateful for their freedom from bondage, they wrapped their arms around the warriors and happily came home. As for the Lakota women, the Oglala would have nothing to do with them and left them without husbands and fathers for their children. It was the honorable and fair thing to do and was the bidding of Mi-Way-To, who upon his father's death, ruled the tribe for the next sixty years with the wisdom of the earth, sun, fire, and rain.

194 Red Patch Road

Since the last couple had moved away over nine months ago, a quiet loneliness edging upon despair had hung over the property. The house sat a half mile off the main road in the rolling hills of eastern Pennsylvania, tucked back behind an old split-rail fence and was surrounded on the southeastern edge of the property by a stone wall that had been constructed by the earliest of the American colonists. There were apple and peach orchards and sweet red and black berry vines that grew wild across the ten acres of the estate. The house originally built back in the 1850's, still remained, but in truth, the only thing that was original was the basement after the fire of 1936. Since then, there had been remodels done to various parts of the house, including the kitchen, living room, bathrooms, and bedrooms. For all intents and purposes, the only two original structures on the property were the basement, which the contractors had used to build upon after the fire, and a large two-story red brick barn that was on its fourth roof.

Today had been an unusual day. A newly married couple had come to look at the property. The two had fallen in love with the house as easily as they had with each other. The real oak floors just needed some sanding and staining, the Victorian cupola just needed some painting, the stone wall just needed some tending to with some mortar, and the large porch would be perfect for lazing about on quiet weekends. Each of them could already envision what swing they were going to purchase and how they would swing on it together. Furthermore, the barn would be perfect for when they saved some money and bought themselves some horses. It would be a labor of love that they could work on together with all the boundless exuberance that a young couple feels in their hearts. That is, except for the basement. It felt as old as the dirt that surrounded it and smelled like it as well. It housed an ancient vegetable cellar, the hot water heater, and the furnace, and then, there was brick on the west wall that the chimney in the main living room originated from. It was the one thing that the couple did not agree upon.

That night, inside their small apartment, the couple spoke about the house. They had been looking for houses for months, and everyone they found was either too small, too expensive, too cheaply made, or in a bad neighborhood. This would be their first house, and they wanted the perfect escape for them and their soon-to-be growing family. It had taken them almost two years to save up a modest down payment of ten thousand dollars and that was with both of them working, but now Clara

Mae was pregnant. It had been around then that Richard, upon getting lost on returning home from a business trip, had stumbled on the old farmhouse, a real gem in the rough. Yes, it needed a lot of care and hard work, but it was priced almost thirty thousand dollars below market value! It had big open rooms, spacious views of the surrounding countryside, and even a small stream at the back of the property. They could see that it was in a bit of disrepair, but the both of them were young and not afraid of hard work. Also, once they fixed it up, they could see the house gaining so much value. The only problem was the basement.

Both of them detested it, but it wasn't a deal breaker for Richard, and eventually, after a bunch of coaxing from him, she relented. He told her anything he could think of to get her to go along with him so that they could purchase the house. He could fix it up. She didn't have to go down there. These houses always had these types of musty basements. She was just being overly sensitive because she was pregnant. The litany of rationalizations, including the amount of money they would make on the property, along with how nice they would make it, finally convinced Clara Mae that the house would do for them and their unborn child.

It was raining the day that they finally moved in. It had started as a light drizzle in the morning and just continued on throughout the day. The early morning haze and mist never burned off, the clouds hanging low well into the evening. It was a dreary day, but one full of excitement for the new homeowners. Boxes, mattresses, televisions, clothing, and so much more was moved into their new residence. At the end of the day, with just the kitchen stuff unpacked so that a light dinner could be prepared, the family dog, Lizzie, was brought in. Taking off across the fields, their three-year-old schnauzer was ecstatic. For an hour, the dog romped and played and scouted out its new domain, carefully marking each square of its property. Then, it was time to go inside the house. The dog visited each room in under five minutes until it reached the door of the basement, and then, it sat down and growled. The couple was shocked. They had known Lizzie since she was a puppy and never even knew that she could growl.

See, it was growling at me.

I moved through the wall behind and blew on its face. Still growling, it began backing up from the door and then turned tail and ran back to its owners. I could see Clara Mae's face, a mask of horror, as she stared at the closed door to the basement, while Richard, standing behind her, appeared confused and concerned. I slipped back through the wall, passing my energy into the electrical wires and, thanks to the day's rain and condensation, proceeded to flicker the lights throughout the house. This was my sanctuary, my purgatory, and, most of all, my house!

I could hear the wails and broken sobs of the wife, and intermittently, the consoling words of the husband resounding. That is when the husband approached the door of the basement.

"This is ridiculous. Come on Lizzie, let's go explore the basement. There is nothing down here but a musty basement. Come on girl."

His voice had changed to a bright sunny flower to try and entice the dog to follow him, but it wasn't going to follow him. Under his breath, he had a few choice words for the dog, but it wasn't going to stop him or his false bravado from going down the stairs. He tried the light switch to turn on the single hanging bulb that illuminated the lower part of the stairs, but it was blown out. There was still a fair amount of light outside, so cautiously, he made his way down the wooden stairs while holding on to the railing. But the third step from the bottom was wet from a small leak in the wall. Descending, apprehensive, and about to reach the bottom of the stairway, an old oil can that had been shelved on top of the furnace conveniently toppled to the ground, rattling over concrete, breaking the eerie stillness.

The misstep on the wet stair hurtled him forward, and as he grabbed ahold of the railing, the screws that held it into the wall came loose, and he was flung down the remaining stairs. As he was falling and attempting to regain his balance, he could see that directly in front of him was a pitchfork that had been placed tines upward against the adjacent wall. In that moment, I could see his face, all contorted and angered and pocked full of furious lines. He could hear his wife screaming as the dog began wildly barking, and only with the best of skill did he manage to grab the handle of the pitchfork prior to being skewered. After hitting his head on the wall in front of him, he lay twisted, in a heap, dazed and aghast at what had just happened. Shooting pain came, and he realized his ankle hurt and that his wife was next to him. She helped him up out of the basement and up the stairs. Over the coming weeks, neither of them spoke to each other about what nearly happened in the basement. The subject had become taboo for them, but from that day forward, the basement door was locked shut.

A few months passed by without further incident. A gate had been put up to stop Lizzie from going down the hallway to the basement door so that Clara Mae did not have to hear the dog's growling, although, ostensibly, it was bought early for the protection of the baby yet to come. Richard's sprained ankle healed, the new paint on the cupola was a fresh white with an Ardennes forest green border, the new porch swing built by the Amish looked perfect from the road, and the freshly mortared stone wall made the yard look well kempt.

After the accident, Clara Mae had been fearful of living in the house and had voiced her complaints to her husband, but like everything, with time and no further disturbances, she was able to block it from her mind. So when Richard was going to be gone on a business trip for two days, she masked her feelings and let him know she would miss him and to call every day. She did not dare make a fuss about the basement because she knew it was a sensitive topic between them. But it lay there in the back of her mind, scarred on her psyche, virtually unchanged from the day they had moved into the house.

It was the first day that Richard was gone, and she had decided to go for a walk through the fields first thing in the morning. Lizzie romped alongside her, and the two of them had a joyous start to the day. The air was fragrant with the smells of flowering trees, insects were buzzing about, and the birds were chirping in song, especially the yellow warblers that were abundant in this part of the country. After an hour, they returned to the house and sat out on the porch swing, the dog with her head on Clara Mae's lap, and her sipping lemonade while enjoying the view of the lush green hills and flowering plants. Later, she brought Lizzie inside to eat, and she turned her attention to the previous night's dishes that were still piled high in the sink. She noticed it was getting harder for her to reach the sink with her belly protruding out so much. She smiled to herself, thinking about the little joy that was in her belly. She caught herself daydreaming and finished the dishes and decided to make herself a snack. She was either famished or stuffed, being that she was pregnant. When she had finished her apple and granola bar, she decided it was time to get herself a quick nap and relax the muscles in her lower back.

She awoke in a start. It was like waking up from a bad dream although she couldn't remember anything bad at all. She could tell she had been sleeping for a while by the light that was streaming through the partially shaded window. A smell, like burning, like sulfur, like ammonia, like something was amiss, floated past. Did she leave the oven on? She was having a hard time thinking, still being in sleep's grasps. Clutching her nightgown, she put on her slippers and walked out into the kitchen.

Here, the smell was stronger, almost acrid. Checking on the oven, she could see it was turned off. Turning, she knew exactly where the smell was coming from. Unmoved, she stared at the entrance to the hallway where the stairs to the basement led. Oh God, why now while Richard was gone? It could be something serious with the furnace or a gas leak. And where was Lizzie? Calling out to her dog, she heard some sounds of what sounded like her dog from below her feet, down in the basement. Quickly, she moved to the hallway entrance. The gate to stop Lizzie from going down the hallway was on the floor, and the door, which had been locked shut for the past two months, was wide open! Lizzie was in the basement.

Hurrying to the door, the stench of sulfur hit her nose, making it crinkle. She grabbed her nightgown and pulled a piece of it over her nose and began the descent into the basement for only the second time in her life. Her husband had replaced the banister railing and patched the leaky wall about a month ago, but hadn't ventured back since. Clutching the railing, she inched her way down the stairs and, at the bottom, picked up a long piece of wood that had been used to prop open one of the small basement windows. The furnace was in the center of the room, and she needed to check on it. With her back to the wall, she inched her way along its side, with her eyes checking in every direction for whatever was lurking within the confines of that damn basement. Her heart was racing, palms were sweating. She tried to whistle for the dog but couldn't get a peep out of her mouth. It was too dry. Finally, she got to the furnace and noticed the pilot light was out. What a relief. Plus, she had even remembered to bring down a lighter. Good, the problem was fixed. This stuff about ghosts and haunted places was nonsense after all. Bending down, she pushed the lighter into the furnace and got it relit. Standing back up again, she turned around, and in the mirror on the far wall was the shadowy appearance of a man in a Civil War uniform standing almost directly behind her on the other side of the furnace. He had wet deep crimson blood on his uniform and was scowling. She remembered screaming but not fainting.

Later that day, dazed and confused with a bump on her head, she awoke to find herself on the floor of the basement next to the furnace. Immediately, she remembered everything that had happened. She peeked around her surroundings and also at the mirror. Luckily, it was just her staring back. A bit disoriented, she began walking out of the cellar, but instead found herself in the vegetable cellar. And that was where she found Lizzie, with her head wedged under one of the slats that made up the floor of the room, lifeless and still, with just the slightest bit of dried blood having escaped from her tiny nose. Gasping for air, hyperventilating and holding her belly, she rushed out of the basement.

A few miles down the street, a local resident found her walking along the side of the road. She was wearing one slipper and was babbling about the demons that lived with her and how they had killed her dog. Unable to find out where she lived, the man who picked her up brought her to the police station, where one of the deputies in the neighborhood recognized her, but just barely. She was only twenty-five years old, but appeared as if she had aged fifteen years within a day. Her hair, once the color of brown chestnuts, had turned an ashen gray color, and her eyes continued to dart about like those of a wild animal that had been captured, all while she spewed crazy things and shouted out obscenities to nobody in general.

Private Dix of the fifteenth Alabama corps, who was shot in the back by a Yankee in 1863 while surrendering at the Battle of Gettysburg, had lived on to claim yet one more unsuspecting victim as he remained trapped in that Pennsylvania farmhouse. The house went back on the market six months later and at way below market value.

The Midnight Murderer

The cicadas pulsed the night air with their incessant mechanical droning, grinding themselves like metal meeting asphalt. They filled the cottonwoods that lined the park, and vaguely sounded like the rental housing units adjacent to them, which had their own version of sexual cacophony. The rental units were abuzz with the noise from the electric neon lights—advertised tattoos, massages and liquor—from the shops below. Both noises reverberated back at each other as the night began, an open invitation for sex or pleasure, deviance or lust. You need to play to win the game, they say.

The streets felt the tread of wanderer after wanderer, loner after loner, tramping about to the rhythm of the cicadas. Palpably, in the stifling air, there could be felt a hunger that needed to be satiated from those who were searching, those who were lost, and those who were hurrying to escape the reality of it all. The pavement let off its steam from the day's heat, and it climbed up the legs of those hungry to fight, fuck, or both. Beneath their feet, the ground bespoke of the city's age and decay, the cracks and lines that lay upon its surface, and the unspoken knowledge that there was nothing anyone could or would do about it. It and the people standing upon it were in a state of disrepair and conspicuously aware of it. Even the cicadas were tainted ghetto whores.

The oppressive heat that wore everything down in its path was starting to wane with the advent of the night clouds, although its oppressiveness still permeated the air, further exacerbated by a sticky wave of pollen that coated everything. The shrieks of the gulls in the parking lot, fighting over torn bread crusts, occasionally broke the still night air, but even their calls sounded tired and wretched. Drug deals for dime bags at the corner were ignored, even by the policeman tired from a long days' worth of talking to the same hoods and getting the same stories. Nobody cared about anyone else's vice, just their own.

Braddock was agitated. There had been seven murders, all women, in less than eight weeks, and he could feel the heat from the brass. He was ensconced in the confines of his air-conditioned police cruiser, with a picture of the Virgin Mary taped below his constantly cracking radio, surveying the grimy scene in front of him. He realized that the only thing different from two months ago, or two years ago for that matter, was the number of hookers on the street. They had lost seven women, strangled, and, sometimes tortured, prior to their deaths. Only four replacements had been seen walking the blocks as far as he could tell. It was like killing cockroaches—you could stamp some of them out, but just like the Immaculate Conception, a few more appeared to take their place within the following days and weeks. Stamping out the butt of his cigarette, he gazed out upon the new girls. They looked scared and apprehensive and still didn't have the "walk" down yet. They strolled too straight up and down. They needed to sway that ass and slink more, like pussy cats do instinctively. He rubbed his chin. Though, who would blame them after what the city had been living through the past few months? A poor city, a hood city, a city on edge that had crumbled from prosperity decades ago, and now, the city had trapped those that were stuck, destined to die amidst the sprawl of its decaying brick buildings.

Slightly, he eased his window down so that he could hear the noise from the streets. Somebody knew who the murderer was, and he wanted to make sure he got wind of anyone who had any inkling of the culprit. The murders had all happened within a twenty-block radius. His twenty-block radius. The precinct chief had a meeting with him about the murders just that morning, a closed-door type, although he had seen how the rest of the precinct staff had scornfully looked at him through the sides of their eyes when he walked toward his office. Somehow they were holding him responsible for the murders. He especially felt the gaze of one of the cockier newer officers in the precinct, Tony Antonoli. By the time he got to the chief's office, he felt like punching that fat peacock in the face. Behind closed doors, the chief wanted to know if he had seen anything. Was there anyone out of the ordinary or new walking the streets? Had he spoken with any of the "johns" or pimps, and what did they think?

The problem was that nobody knew anything, and those who knew either weren't talking or were at the morgue. The lieutenant wasn't satisfied and let him know it in no uncertain terms. The mayor and the community leaders were putting the heat on the lieutenant, which had all just passed on through to Braddock. As a twenty-year veteran of the force, he felt he deserved a little better than to have to come out to a quiet squad room, where he had to avoid the faces of everyone who had been listening to the screaming lieutenant. And the worst part of it all was that he had been saddled with a rookie who didn't know shit.

McGregor had spent the morning getting under his skin. Why aren't we canvassing the streets? Should we do a sting operation? What had he seen over the past two months? Who did he think the killer was? Why were they just sitting in the police car? Finally, exasperated with the young man's line of questioning, he put him on street patrol. Braddock sent the kid away, who, oddly enough, was wearing blue polyester wool blend shirt and trousers, dark black shoes and socks, and woolen cap on a ninety-degree day. That would quiet him down.

"Go check out the Pemberton street area and see what you turn up. Ask any of the hoods if they saw or knew of anything. I will be circling around the area looking for anything suspicious. Then report back to me in an hour," he had told him.

It was at that moment that Gina walked by his car, twirling her sunglasses in her hand and chewing a piece of gum.

"Hey Officer Braddock, got a cigarette for a hard-working girl like me?"

She had been working the area for almost five years now and was past her prime. At one time, she had been quite attractive, with her long auburn hair and perky tits. She had been a former dancer at Mike's topless lounge a few years back when she was younger, and her good looks could get the men to stuff dollars in her bikini strap. But like almost all prostitutes, she had gotten hooked on drugs. The meth had dragged away her good looks and replaced them with shaky hands, skin blotches, and lines along her cheeks that would have made you mistake her for a woman in her fifties. She was barely thirty and dying young.

Braddock looked up at her through the slit in the window and smiled. Whenever he looked at her, he couldn't think of what a shame. A long time ago, when he was a rookie, like McGregor was now, he might have tried to talk to the prostitutes and show them the evil of their ways and get them into a rehab clinic. But not anymore. Lowering his window so that it was fully open, he stuffed his hand in his front pocket and took out a pack of menthol cigarettes. Deftly moving the cigarette pack toward her through the open window, he ever so slightly jerked his hand so that one instantly protruded from the end. Even with the added help, her shaky hands had trouble getting to the offered cigarette.

"What's the news on the street, Gina?"

"Everybody's scared Braddock. I can't even get any business because the regulars are anxious about getting picked up and blamed for the murders."

She lit the cigarette and took a long drag off of it. He could tell she was fixating on her next hit of meth and didn't have the funds. The realization hit him then: She was so desperate that she was willing to continue walking the streets for cash, even knowing that a serial killer was preying upon women like her. Then again, what choice did she actually have at her disposal? It wasn't like she could lay low and relax in her comfortable house or go on vacation. The only thing she owned that was of any value was between her legs, and that asset was depreciating rapidly.

"Why don't you take yourself to a shelter and check in for a few days?"

"Already tried that. They are filled up and don't want anyone on drugs anyway. I'll take my chances. I know how to handle myself," she said with a crooked half smile.

Wanting to stretch his legs, Braddock exited the patrol car but looked down at the ground as she smiled, not wanting to look at her as he threw his cigarette butt to the pavement and ground it with his boot. He had enjoyed watching her at Mike's years back, and she knew it, but nowadays, it made him sick to see what the drugs had done to her, and he couldn't return the smile knowing he would be looking back at brown stained yellowing teeth surrounded by a drawn, crinkled face. A sense of utter despair pulled at his heart. Pulling twenty dollars from his pocket, he stuffed it into her prematurely withered hand and saw the pupils of her eyes light up, if only for an instant.

"Grab something to eat, will you?"

He saw her clutching the bill so tightly he imagined her fingernails driving into the palm of her hand.

"Braddock, you are the best! I know you have arrested me in the past, and we have had our differences, but you are one standup guy. All the girls know that. God bless you! And I hope you catch that psycho killer!"

And with that, she was gone. But certainly not toward any restaurant. She was headed directly for the dope man, the doctor, the anxiety reliever and pain killer. Twenty would put her right for all night. Like a breeze that is gone in an instant, she lunged down the street in search of her destiny. Braddock chuckled to himself. Catch the killer. Sure, he would catch the killer. Looking past the street shops, he recognized McGregor dragging himself back toward him, fighting the oppressive heat and humidity. He certainly wasn't moving as fast as when he had left off earlier in a hurry to catch the killer.

"How did you do? Did you find out anything useful? Were the boys over on Pemberton glad to see you? Have you cracked the case, yet?"

Braddock was beginning to enjoy the needling he was giving the kid after all of the annoying questions that he had to withstand earlier in the day. Directly in front of him stood one of the unhappiest, sweaty, and disgruntled people he had ever seen. He could see that his pants and shirt were sticking to him, with the sweat stains being the most prevalent under his arms, and all across his face and brow, he dripped. It had only taken an hour for the eager beaver to metamorphize into a grumpy bear. The irony was not lost on the rookie.

"Actually, I did find something out. You are a lazy asshole. But besides that, I did find something else out. All of the women were experienced players. The ones that have been knocked off have all been around a long time. You know what I mean?"

"Hmmm . . . You may just have something there. You mean the killer likes used poontang. I think if we get that out on an APB, we might just have our man within a few hours. I bet the lieutenant is really going to be proud of you for figuring this one out."

"You know what . . . just fuck off Braddock. I have been working with you for exactly a half a day now, and I can already see right through you and your type. At least I am trying to solve this case while you are sitting on your fat ass sucking down cigarettes. Mister high and mighty getting overtime to sit in an air-conditioned car, dreaming of retirement."

Braddock sat in the driver's side of the cruiser and bobbed his head up and down.

"Sure kid, you know me, and you know my type. I bet you scored a hundred percent on all your psychology exams while going through basic training and can't wait to show off all your knowledge. I tell you what, while you're working with me, just can it."

It was at that instant a car blew by them going sixty in a thirty-five zone. Braddock clicked on his police siren and whipped out after the offender. It wasn't much of a bust. A mother, late to pick up her son at school, and damn near in tears by the time Braddock had reached the car. He had McGregor run her license, which came back clean except for a speeding ticket from three years ago. He could tell she was scraping by moneywise from the condition of her car and how she was dressed, and he knew a second speeding ticket in three years was going to jack her insurance. Handing back her license, he let her off with a warning. He had bigger fish to fry anyway. When he had pulled her over, the local drug pusher, Slim Billy, was standing on the corner, enjoying the spectacle of someone else being caught and busted by the cops.

"Hey Billy, come over here."

The smile disappeared from Billy's face. McGregor, who was beginning to protest the issuance of a warning rather than a ticket, stopped short. He looked perplexed. Billy sauntered over to them as the woman in the car was just getting ready to drive off.

"Excuse me miss. For just a moment, please refrain from driving off."

Braddock, in a motion like a pit bull striking, grabbed Billy by his long hair, slamming his face into the hood of the car while bending his arm back behind his back.

"Now, do you know why you are in trouble? Gina was part of a sting operation, and I bet you have her marked twenty-dollar bill in your pocket."

With his left hand still firmly holding Billy's arm behind his back, nose dribbling blood onto the car hood, he stuffed his hand into Billy's jeans and came out with a wad of cash. Leafing through the cash while McGregor put handcuffs on Billy, he spotted what he was looking for, the twenty he had given Gina not twenty minutes prior.

"Well looky here. I have myself proof you just sold her drugs. Looks like you are going to jail."

Billy began yelling and screaming. This was police brutality, a sham set up by a low-life police officer, and the department was going to hear from his lawyer. All of his ministrations got him nowhere. Braddock opened the cruiser's back door and pushed Billy into the back seat, but not before grabbing ahold of his t-shirt and yanking a piece of it off of him. With the piece of cloth in his hand, he proceeded to the woman's car and wiped off the blood.

"You are free to go miss. Let this be a warning to you to drive carefully. We don't want to hurt any of our up-standing citizens here, like Billy, who hang out on street corners."

By this time, a small crowd had gathered and were watching with eagle-eyed amusement. For many of them, this was the highlight of their evening. Over the din of the traffic noise, people could still hear Billy yelling in the back of the squad car as he thrashed about with his ripped shirt. By the time Braddock got back in the car, Billy had exhausted his lungs. The three of them drove away in silence. As they passed an abandoned field, Braddock slowed down and stopped. McGregor looked over at him with curiosity. Braddock got out of the car and walked around to the back of the squad car and yanked Billy out. Billy was looking at him with a strange, scared look in his eyes.

"What are you doing?"

Braddock had already un-holstered his gun and had it pointed at Billy.

"Hey man, what the fuck do you want from me?"

McGregor, not believing his eyes, his jaw somewhere down around the middle of his neck, tried to get out of the car, but he was locked in. Braddock could hear McGregor screaming in the car to let him out as he fumbled with the door latch. So there Braddock was, with a gun pointed at Billy, McGregor behind him locked in his own squad car, and both of them frantic, not knowing what was going to happen next. Billy heard the trigger cock back and saw McGregor desperately attempting to get out of the car.

"Please don't kill me man. Don't kill me. Don't kill me. I promise I won't sell anymore drugs. I will move away. I promise. I mean it man, I promise. Just don't kill me."

Billy was bawling like a baby, the tears running down his cheeks. With the gun in his left hand, Braddock unzipped his pants and proceeded to urinate all over Billy's right pants leg and shoes. Then, he re-holstered his gun and undid the cuffs about Billy's wrists.

"If I ever see you again in my precinct, I will give you your last one-way ride. Do you understand?"

Billy ran a lot faster than Braddock thought he was capable of. He made a mental note of it. Upon zipping up his pants, he unlocked the car and eased his way into the driver's seat. The air was thick within the cruiser's cabin on the trip back to the station as McGregor seethed.

Back at the station, McGregor bolted for the lieutenant and cornered him within his office. Behind closed doors, but viewable to all through the glass walls, the station house witnessed an extremely agitated and animated McGregor act out the scenes of what had just transpired in Precinct 53. After he was finished, Lieutenant Miller called out for Braddock to step into his office. With everyone in the station watching his every move, he calmly got up from his desk, picked up his coffee, and folded the newspaper he was reading under his arm. He then strode through the office like he was on a Sunday morning stroll. He sat down opposite the lieutenant's desk and placed his folded newspaper and coffee before him.

"All right Braddock, let's have it. McGregor says you hit a suspect, let a woman go who was carelessly speeding in a residential area, locked him in the squad car, and threatened to kill Billy while robbing him! Oh, wait a minute, I forgot to mention that he also said you urinated on the aforementioned suspect. Now, would you mind filling me in on this morning's escapades before I have you shining shoes down at headquarters!"

God, Miller always put on a good act for the troops. I mean if he was supposed to be mad—well he looked mad, and boy did he ever look mad. But he knew Miller. Miller was putting on a show for the boys so that they could see there was some semblance of order and that the power structure was intact, so that in the back of everyone's mind when they got home and shined their badge before going off to Neverland, it meant there was justice in the world.

"Lieutenant did I ever tell you what a fine job I think you do when you yell at us? I mean, it really helps the morale around here to think that someone actually cares about their job. It is no wonder why they made you lieutenant."

"Cut the crap Braddock and stop trying to butter me up!"

"Well . . . first of all, I always let you know not to send me out with green horns, and that is exactly what you did. In any case, he has it all backward. First of all, for his own protection, I locked him in the car while I relieved myself along the side of the road. Therefore, since he wasn't with me while I was letting Billy go, I was forced to keep my gun on the suspect prior to his release, since, like I said, I was relieving myself. Unfortunately, I had too many cups of coffee at Mario's this morning."

Braddock paused and sipped his coffee before continuing, "Anyways, like I was saying, if some of it happened to splash on Billy, then so be it, but that deliberate stuff is nonsense. I was holding a gun and pissing at the same time while interrogating my suspect. That is not an easy thing to do, mind you. I was multitasking while protecting my newest partner. And that stuff about me robbing him is ridiculous. I set up a sting and took the bait money back, and the only reason that I had to bloody and cuff Billy was that he started to pull something out of his waist line, which very well could have been a gun. These are things that rookies just don't see until it's too late and they're lining a casket. And if I am supposed to write a ticket for every person who speeds around this God for-saken town, then half of city hall and your bosses would be at Saturday driving school."

"So that's how it is, huh?"

"Exactly as I see it."

The slits where Miller's eyes used to be said every-thing about how he felt. In between the two stories was the truth, somewhere between the cavalier approach of the long-journeyed lawman and the new man fighting for complete, unadulterated justice. He knew that both of their own perverted senses of right and wrong were at opposite ends of the spectrum, but none of this chicken shit nonsense was getting him anywhere. Furthermore, it was wasting his time, and more importantly, they were no closer to solving the murders.

By the time Braddock had left the chief's office, Mil-ler had decided to take up an offer from the Central In-telligence Department. They had offered up one of their female officers to act as a decoy. She would start work-ing as a prostitute. She was fairly new and nobody from Precinct 53 would know of her, and that anonymity would let her double as his spy on the streets to see what his officers were really doing. Her name was Victoria Jackson.

The newspapers had named the killer the "Midnight Murderer." All of the victims had been killed between ten at night and two in the morning and then unceremoniously dumped into the Mohegan River, which ran through the roughest sections of town down by the old steel mills and coal processing plants. Many of the bodies washed ashore downstream, where the water got more shallow and natural eddies would occur, thereby trapping the bodies. By the following morning, an eddy had trapped another victim. Gina's body had been found floating just south of town, naked and strangled to death.

Victoria Jackson began working the beat. New to town, she understood that her role as an undercover police officer, decoy, and double agent carried with it inherent risks, but she had accepted the position. Eight women were dead, and this fiend was still out there. Without this type of work, he would never be stopped. She was wearing a wire and had been assured that if any situation got dangerous, backup would be there in less than five minutes. Still, knowing that it took a lot less than five minutes to strangle someone to death, she was on guard. So far, she had been working a week without any luck, and this night had been uneventful as well. It was three in the morning when she decided her shift was over. She began walking back to her car. That was when the police car pulled up in front of her. With the white spotlight directed at her face, she couldn't see anything.

"You are under arrest for solicitation of sex."

She stopped dead in her tracks. What was this? Some type of bad joke? She heard a car door open and shut and saw a large man approaching her.

"Wait a minute there, buddy, I am . . ."

And at that moment, still blinded by the spotlight, she felt her arm viciously tugged as she was spun around and put into a chokehold by the officer, and her other arm was lifted behind her back, immobilizing her. She felt herself trying to scream, but no sounds were coming from her throat. The feeling of being completely helpless as she was dragged to the car was new to her and devastatingly frightening. She knew she may have only one chance to save herself. But she was ready for him. When he took his hand off of her arm to open the car door, she was able to spin around on him and knee him in the groin. He grunted with pain and exhaled, but he had been ready for her as well. She felt the electricity burning through her body, her veins, her muscles, and head like she had touched lightning. Once before, she had been tagged with electricity while in training at the academy. Her whole body went limp and numb, and there was no controlling any of her bodies' functions. She collapsed on the street.

In the back seat of the car, she found herself bound and gagged and still trembling from having 10,000 volts of electricity run through her body. She had lost her shoes, and her skirt was completely wet from having peed on herself. Vaguely, she realized he was speaking to her.

"Feisty one you are. I bet you thought you were going to leave me screaming on the ground with that knee of yours. You dumb bitch . . . that is why we wear cups."

He was quiet for a while as they drove toward the outskirts of the city. Then, he pulled off the road at a deserted warehouse and grabbed her from the back of the car. She didn't have much fight left in her after being tasered and was looking and hoping for an opportunity to escape. Soon enough, she felt his hands around her neck. She could feel her voice box being crushed. There was not much she could do to fight back with her arms and feet being bound, but she squirmed and fought with everything thing she had, even if she knew it was hopeless. As she began to pass out, she remembered being let go of and falling to the ground, hearing a loud bang, and finally hitting her head on something very hard.

***

Later, after being revived at the hospital, she was told the story of how she survived. When the lieutenant had heard her being arrested over the wire, he had sent out all of his squad cars in pursuit. There was only supposed to be two patrol cars in the area, and one of them was arresting her. Both had radioed back, letting them know they were in pursuit, which meant that a third patrol car, an off-duty policeman, was the culprit. When Braddock arrived at the warehouse after tailing them, he parked and entered the abandoned warehouse. What happened next was a tragedy not only for the police department and those it was supposed to serve and protect, but also for the eight women found in the Mohegan River. Braddock found Antolini strangling Victoria Jackson. When he turned around, Antolini momentarily let her go, and went for his gun. In the split-second instant it took him to raise his gun to shoot, a bullet went straight through his chest. The "Midnight Murderer" had been relieved of duty, permanently.

Coming Soon!

Exterminator 69
by
John Tanner

Mick Tanner, also known as exterminator 69, was on the job, bored out of his mind, and had started talking to himself again. Unfortunately, talking to himself was beginning to become something of a habit. Being an exterminator on call to kill bugs was like waiting for Santa Claus. Until…

For more information
visit: www.SpeakingVolumes.us

On Sale Now!

**For more information
visit:** www.SpeakingVolumes.us